Dear Reader,

Looking back over the years, I find it hard to realise that twenty-six of them have gone by since I wrote my first book—*Sister Peters in Amsterdam*. It wasn't until I started writing about her that I found that once I had started writing, nothing was going to make me stop—and at that time I had no intention of sending it to a publisher. It was my daughter who urged me to try my luck.

I shall never forget the thrill of having my first book accepted. A thrill I still get each time a new story is accepted. Writing to me is such a pleasure, and seeing a story unfolding on my old typewriter is like watching a film and wondering how it will end. Happily of course.

To have so many of my books re-published is such a delightful thing to happen and I can only hope that those who read them will share my pleasure in seeing them on the bookshelves again. . .and enjoy reading them.

Back by Popular Demand

A collector's edition of favourite titles from one of the world's best-loved romance authors. Mills & Boon are proud to bring back these sought after titles and present them as one cherished collection.

BETTY NEELS: COLLECTOR'S EDITION

UNCERTAIN SUMMER

BY
BETTY NEELS

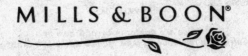

MILLS & BOON®

MILLS & BOON and MILLS & BOON with the Rose Device
are registered trademarks of the publisher.

First published in Great Britain 1972 by Mills & Boon Limited
This edition 1999
Harlequin Mills & Boon Limited,
Eton House, 18-24 Paradise Road, Richmond, Surrey TW9 1SR

© Betty Neels 1972

ISBN 0 263 80695 2

Set in Times Roman 10 on 11 pt by
Rowland Phototypesetting Limited
Bury St Edmunds, Suffolk

73-9905-56836

Made and printed in Great Britain by
Caledonian International Book Manufacturing Ltd, Glasgow

CHAPTER ONE

THE April sun was bright and warm even at the early
hour of half past seven in the morning; it shone
through the window of Serena Potts' bedroom in the
Nurses' Home, on to her bright head of dark hair
which she was crowning somewhat impatiently with
her cap. The cap was a pretty trifle, spotted muslin
and frilled and worn with strings, but she had tied
these in a hurry, so that the bow beneath her pretty
chin was a trifle rakish. She gave it an angry tweak,
anchored the cap more firmly and raced from the
room, along the long bare corridor and down two
flights of stairs, into the covered way leading to the
hospital, to arrive a minute or so later, out of breath,
at the breakfast table.

Her arrival was greeted by cries of surprise by
the young women already seated there, but she took
no notice of these until she had poured her tea,
shaken cornflakes into a bowl and sat herself down.

'No need to carry on so, just because I'm early,'
she pointed out equably. 'Staff's away and there's
only the first-year students and Harris on, and you
know what Hippy's like if anything comes in a
second after seven-thirty.' She raised her dark,
thickly lashed eyes piously and intoned primly:

'You are aware, are you not, Sister Potts, that I
will accept no responsibility for any cases brought
into the Accident Room after half past seven pre-
cisely?'

She began to bolt down the cornflakes. 'I bet

5

the floors will be strewn with diabetic comas and overdoses by the time I get there, and Harris will be arguing with everyone within sight.'

She buttered toast rapidly, weighed it down with marmalade and bit into it, and everyone at the table murmured sympathetically—at one time or another they had all had Nurse Harris to work for them—a scholarly girl, with no sense of humour and a tendency to stand and argue over a patient when what was really needed was urgent resuscitation. Serena found it difficult to bear with her, just as she found Sister Hipkins difficult. Hippy was getting on for fifty and one of the team of Night Sisters at Queen's, and while she was adequate enough on the medical side, she was hopeless in Casualty and the Accident Room; besides, accidents had a nasty habit of arriving just as she was about to go off duty, and she was a great one for going off punctually.

Serena wolfed the rest of her toast, swallowed tea in great unladylike gulps, said 'bye-bye' a little indistinctly and went off briskly to the Accident Room.

It, and Casualty, occupied the whole of the ground floor of one wing of the hospital. Each had its own Sister in charge, but as the two young ladies in question took their days off on alternate week-ends, it meant that today being Monday, Serena would be in charge of both departments until Betsy Woods, who had Cas, returned at one o'clock. She swung into the waiting-room now, casting a practised but kindly eye over the few people already seated on the benches. She recognized several of them; workers from one of the nearby factories, apparently accident-prone, with cuts and grazes clutching their tetanus cards in their hands as proof positive that they were up-to-date with their anti-tetanus injections and thus free from what they invariably referred to as the needle.

Serena wished them a cheerful good morning, stopped with no sign of impatience when she was begged to stop by an old woman who wished her to look at an injured eye, and having done this, offered sympathy and the mendacious information that the doctor would be along in a few minutes, and sped on her way again. Bill Travers, the Casualty Officer, had been up most of the night, Staff Nurse Watts had whispered to her as she met her at the door, and the chance of him appearing much before nine o'clock was so unlikely as to be laughable, but the old woman had needed comfort. She crossed the vast waiting-room to the Accident Room entrance and met Sister Hipkins coming out of it.

'And high time too, Sister Potts,' said Hippy nastily. 'No staff nurse and an RTA in! I'm sure I don't know what you young women are coming to—in my young days I wouldn't have dared to be late.'

'I'm not late,' said Serena with resigned calm. 'It's not quite ten to eight, I'm due on at eight o'clock, and you are off duty at the same time—I don't know where you get the idea that you're off duty at half past seven, Sister Hipkins.'

She didn't wait for an answer, but went on past Hippy, oblivious of her furious look, intent on getting to the case before Nurse Harris had a chance to do her worst.

The Accident Room was semi-circular, with screened-off bays and a vast central area to allow for the rapid manoeuvrings of trolleys and stretchers and the easy passage of the doctors and nurses. The curtains had been drawn across the furthest bay and she started towards it, her eyes searching the department as she went, to make sure that everything was in its proper place.

Nurse Harris was standing by the patient, looking important, and while doing nothing herself, issuing orders to the other two more junior nurses with her. Serena promised herself ten minutes with Nurse Harris later on, said calmly, 'Good morning, everybody,' and went to look at the patient—a man, young, and unconscious, presumably from the head wound visible through his blond hair. Serena took his pulse and pupil reaction and told the more senior of the two nurses to start cleaning the wound.

'His leg,' breathed Harris importantly, 'it's broken.'

Serena drew back the blanket covering the young man and saw the splints the ambulance men had put on. As she did so she asked:

'Did Sister Hipkins tell you to ring anyone?'

'No, Sister.'

'Then ring Mr Thompson'—he was the RSO—'ask him to come down here, please, and tell him it's an RTA. Head wound, probable fracture of left leg—badly shocked, unconscious.' And when Harris didn't move, she added with a patience she didn't feel, 'Will you hurry, Nurse, and then come back to me here.'

She was cutting the outside seam of the torn trousers covering the injured leg by the time Harris got back. She was doing it very carefully because if it was properly done, the trousers could be repaired. Experience had taught her that not everyone had the money to buy new trousers, although this man looked prosperous enough; she had noted the gold wrist watch and cuff links, the silk shirt and the fine tweed of his suit, and his shoes were expensive.

'Make out an X-ray form, Nurse,' she told Harris, 'and one for the Path Lab too—I daresay they'll want to do a crossmatch. What about relatives?'

Harris looked blank, and Serena, holding back impatience, asked:

'His address—you've got that? Was he conscious when they got to him?'

'Yes, Sister. But Sister Hipkins said we weren't to disturb him when he was brought in, and the ambulance men didn't know, because he was only conscious for a few minutes when they reached him.'

Serena counted silently to ten, because when she was a little girl, her father had taught her to do that, so that her temper, which was, and still was, hot at times, could cool. It was a silly childish trick, but it worked. She said with no trace of ill-humour: 'Go and make sure the trolleys are ready, Nurse, will you? then bring in the stitch trolley.'

Later, she promised herself, she would go and see the Number Seven, Miss Stokes, and see if something could be done to get Harris off the department. Her eyes flickered to the clock. Two part-time staff nurses would be on at nine o'clock, and thank heaven for them, she thought fervently. She had the splint off now with the most junior of the nurses helping her, and turned to wish Mr Thompson a friendly good morning as he came in.

He was a thin young man with a permanently worried expression on his pleasant face, but he was good at his job. 'I thought you might want to take a look at this head before the orthopaedic man gets here,' explained Serena. 'Sorry to get you down so early, Tom.'

He smiled nicely at her and set to work to examine

the patient. 'Nice-looking bloke,' he commented as he explored the scalp wound. 'Do we know who he is?'

'Not yet. . .'

'Unconscious when they found him?'

'No—not all the time, and he was conscious for a very short time when he got here.'

He gave her an understanding look. 'Hippy on last night?'

Serena nodded. 'I'll go through his pockets as soon as you've been over him.'

'Um,' agreed Mr Thompson. 'Where's this leg?'

She whisked back the blanket and pointed with a deceptively useless-looking little hand. There was a discoloured bump just above the ankle and a sizeable bruise. 'Pott's,' she said succinctly. 'Now you're here I'll get this shoe off.'

Mr Thompson obligingly held the leg steady while she eased it off and after he had taken a closer look said: 'You're right—X-ray, and we'd better see to that head too. I'll do it now, shall I? It only needs a couple of stitches, so if everything's ready I'll get down to it, then Orthopaedics can take over when he's been X-rayed.'

Serena waved a hand at the small trolley Harris had wheeled in. 'Help yourself. Do you want a local? He might come to.'

She looked down at the man on the examination table and encountered bright blue eyes staring at her. He smiled as he spoke, but she was unable to understand a word. She smiled back at him and said to no one in particular: 'Foreign—I wonder what he said?'

Her query was answered by the patient. 'I will translate. I said: "What a beautiful little gipsy girl." '

His English was almost without accent. He smiled again and watched admiringly while Serena's dark beauty became even more striking by reason of the colour which crept slowly over her cheeks. It was Mr Thompson's chuckle, turned too late into a cough, which prompted her to say coolly, despite her discomfiture: 'We should like your name and address, please, so that we can let your family know. Could you manage to tell us?'

He closed his eyes and for a moment she thought he had drifted off into unconsciousness again, but he opened them again.

'Van Amstel, Zierikzee, Holland,' he said. 'Anyone will know. . .' He turned his eyes on Mr Thompson. 'What's wrong?' he asked. 'I'm a doctor, so presumably I may be told.'

Mr Thompson told him. 'I'm going to stitch that scalp wound,' he went on, 'then you'll have an X-ray. We'll have to see about the leg too.'

'I must stay here?'

'I'm afraid so—for the moment at least.'

The young man looked at Serena again. 'I find nothing to be afraid of myself,' he said. 'On the contrary.' He stared at Serena, who returned his look with a bright professional smile which successfully hid her interest; he really was remarkably good-looking, and although she was a kind-hearted girl, and felt genuine sympathy for the patients who passed through her capable hands on their way to hospital beds, just for once she found herself feeling pleased that Doctor van Amstel should be forced to stay in hospital. She reflected with satisfaction that she was on excellent terms with the Surgical Floor Sister; she would be able to find out more about him. Her hands, as busy as her thoughts, passed Mr

Thompson the local anaesthetic, all ready drawn up as she told one of the nurses to get the porters. 'X-ray, Nurse, and please go with the patient. He'll be coming back here to see the Orthopaedic side afterwards.'

She was spraying the wound with nebucutane when the patient spoke again. 'Sister, will you telephone my cousin? Ask for Zierikzee—the exchange will know—it's a small place, there'll be no difficulty.'

'Has your cousin the same name?'

'Yes, he's a doctor too.'

Serena nodded. 'Very well, I'll do it while you're in X-ray. Am I to say anything special?'

He frowned a little. 'No—just tell him.' He closed his eyes again and as he was wheeled away Mr Thompson said: 'Nasty crack on the head. Was it his fault?'

Serena led the way to her office and found the note the ambulance men had thoughtfully left for her. She found a policeman too, who wanted to see the patient and take a statement. She left Mr Thompson to talk to him while she got the exchange. She was connected with Zierikzee very quickly, and it was only when someone said Hullo that she realized that she didn't know if the cousin understood English. Obedient to her patient's instructions, however, she asked for Doctor van Amstel's house, adding that it was urgent. Apparently the operator understood her, for after a few moments a deep voice said in her ear: 'Doctor van Amstel.'

'Oh,' said Serena foolishly, because she hadn't expected it to be as easy as all that. 'I'm telephoning from London.' She added in a little rush, 'You understand English?'

'I get by,' the voice assured her.

'Well, we have a Doctor van Amstel in our hospital—Queen's. He's had an accident. . .'

'An RTA?' inquired the voice surprisingly.

'Yes.' She hadn't known that Road Traffic Accident was a term used in other countries. 'His car hit a bus.'

'His fault?'

Heartless man, thought Serena, worrying about a mere car when his cousin was injured. 'I've no idea,' she said coldly, and was taken aback when he chuckled.

'All right, Nurse—or is it Sister? Let me know the worst.'

She told him a little tartly and he said: 'Tut-tut, the same leg as last time, but at least it's not an arm this time.'

She asked faintly and against her will: 'Does—does he do this often?'

'Yes. I'll keep in touch, and thank you, Sister—er—?'

'Potts.'

'Incredible. . .goodbye.'

She put down the receiver slowly, wondering why he had said 'incredible' like that. Perhaps his knowledge of English wasn't as good as he would have her believe. A nice voice, though, although he had sounded as though he had been laughing. She dismissed him from her thoughts and turned to the work awaiting her.

There was no skull fracture, said the radiologist, just a nasty crack on the head and a clean break of the tib and fib, but the orthopaedic registrar, pursing his lips over the discoloured swelling, decided to call in Sir William Sandhurst, his consultant, not because he didn't feel more than capable of reducing the fracture and applying the plaster himself, but because the patient was a doctor and rated private patient treatment. For the same reason, Serena was asked to arrange for him to have one of the private rooms on the surgical floor, and thither, after the necessary treatment, the Dutch doctor was borne. Serena was busy by then, dealing with the wide variety of accidents which poured in non-stop during the day, but he had still contrived to ask her if she would go and see him later in the day and she had agreed. Moreover, when she had a moment to herself she had to admit to herself too that she was looking forward to seeing him again.

The morning slipped into the afternoon with the shortest of pauses for dinner because a bad scald came in and she didn't want to leave it; she went with the pathetic, mercifully unconscious child to the Children's Ward and returned to find a policeman bringing in two youths who had been fighting, using broken bottles. Teatime came and went before they were fit to be handed over to the ward. She heaved a sigh of relief as they were wheeled away and the junior nurse, just back from tea, said:

'I'll clear up, Sister. Agnes—' Agnes was the department maid who, between bouts of swabbing floors and washing paint, mothered them all—'has made you some tea, she's taken it into the office.'

Bill Travers had been doing the stitching; he caught Serena by the arm remarking: 'I hope I'm included in the tea party,' and when she declared that of course he was, walked her briskly to the office where the admirable Agnes had not only produced an enormous pot of tea but a plate of buttered toast as well.

As Serena poured out, Bill asked, 'Off at five? Are you going out?'

Serena was annoyed to feel her cheeks getting warm. 'Not just...that is, perhaps—later on.'

Her companion eyed her narrowly. 'What's this I hear from Thompson about the handsome young Dutchman brought in this morning? Called you a beautiful little gipsy, didn't he?'

She looked suitably reproving. 'You are a lot!' she declared wrathfully. 'Nothing but gossip from morning to night!' she snorted delicately. 'He didn't know what he was saying.'

'Come off it, Serena, don't tell me you don't know by now that you *are* a beautiful little gipsy—at least you look like one. He must have been instantly smitten.'

Serena tossed her rather untidy head. 'Nonsense!' She caught her companion's eye and giggled engagingly. 'As a matter of fact, he was rather interesting.'

'And you're going to see him on your way off duty, I suppose? just to make sure Joan Walters isn't pulling a fast one on you? He's on Surgical, I take it.'

'Don't be beastly! Joan's my best friend. I'm only going to see if there's anything I can do—after all, he is a foreigner.'

'That's not going to stop the police asking awkward questions—it was his fault, driving an E-type Jag up a one-way street.'

Serena refilled their cups. 'No? Did he really? Lucky it wasn't a lot worse for him.'

'And that the bus he collided with was a bus and not some defenceless Mini.'

Serena got up. 'Look,' she said reasonably, 'you drive a Mini, and anything less defenceless I've yet to meet—it's nothing but a battering ram once you're in the driver's seat.' She smiled. 'I must get back, Staff White's on in ten minutes and I want to be cleared up before she gets here. There's nothing worse than other people's leftovers when you come on duty.'

She nodded airily and hurried back to make sure that the department was clear once more. She had had a busy day, but she didn't look in the least tired, only untidy, but she was such a pretty girl that a shining nose and a few stray curling ends did nothing to detract from her appearance. She was a slim small girl and this, combined with her outstanding good looks, made it hard for people who didn't know what work she did to believe that she was a nurse. She rolled up her sleeves now as she went, looked at the clock, said: 'Off you go,' to the student nurse who was due off duty, and took the laundry bag from her as she spoke, so that the other nurse could finish filling it with the used linen. They were still hard at it when Staff Nurse White reported for duty.

Serena went off herself ten minutes later, and quite unmindful of her untidy pile of hair and shining nose, went straight to the surgical floor. It was on the other side of the hospital, three stories up, and as she had to cross the main entrance hall to reach it, she took the opportunity of posting some letters in the box by the big glass doors. This done, she paused to look outside; the day was still fine and the busy city street was thronged with traffic and people hurrying home from work. As she watched, a dilapidated Mini drew up, was wedged expertly into the space between two other cars and its driver got out and mounted the few shallow steps before the door without haste. He paused within a foot of her, and she was conscious of his eyes resting upon her for the briefest of moments before he walked, still without haste, across to the porter's lodge. She was left with the impression of size and height and unhurried calm, but by the time she turned round to take another discreet look, there was no sign of him.

She was half-way up the stone staircase to the first floor when she met Miss Stokes coming down. Miss Stokes, who by virtue of the Salmon Scheme had turned from Office Sister Stokes to a Number Seven in the hierarchy of the nursing profession, smiled and stopped. She had been at Queen's for a very long time, long before Serena had arrived there to do her training, six years earlier. She was a pleasant, good-natured body, in whom young nurses willingly confided and with whom the older, more experienced ones conferred.

'Busy day, Sister Potts?' she wanted to know, and sounded as though she were really interested.

'Very, Miss Stokes, and if you can spare a second, when is it convenient to have a word with you?'

'Now,' said Miss Stokes, who was an opportunist by nature.

'Nurse Harris—' began Serena, and her superior nodded understandingly. 'Could she be moved, do you think? She's quite unsuited to Cas work, she— she isn't quite quick enough.'

'I know—I don't know where to put that girl. She's theoretically brilliant and she hasn't even mastered the art of making a patient comfortable. I had hoped that in the Accident Room she would be able to apply her knowledge.'

'She does,' said Serena, ''but the patients can't always wait while she does.'

Miss Stokes allowed herself a smile. 'I can well imagine she's somewhat of a responsibility. I'll move her, Sister, don't worry.'

'Thank you, Miss Stokes.' The two ladies smiled
a farewell to each other and went their separate ways;
Miss Stokes to half an hour's peace and quiet in her
office, Serena to run up another flight of stairs and
go through the swing doors at the top to the surgical
floor. Half-way down the corridor she met one of
the staff nurses and asked her if Sister was around,
and was told that she was, with one of the consultants.

'I've come to see the patient we sent up this morning, Staff—Doctor van Amstel. Is it OK if I go in?'

Staff thought so. 'He's in number twenty-one,
Sister,' she advised her, and darted off with the
faintly harassed air of someone who had a lot to do
and not enough time in which to do it.

Number twenty-one's door was closed, Serena
tapped and went in and came to an abrupt halt just
inside the door because the doctor had a visitor; the
large man who had got out of the dilapidated Mini—
he had draped his length into the only easy chair in
the room and unfolded it now at the sight of her, to
stand silent and faintly smiling. It was the patient
who spoke first.

'I've been waiting for you,' he remarked cheerfully, 'to brighten up an otherwise very dull day.'

'Dull?' Serena was astonished; people who had
car accidents and broke legs and what have you
didn't usually refer to such happenings as dull.

'Oh, yes, only not any more—it's turned out to be
a red letter day, I shouldn't have met you otherwise,
should I?'

She went faintly pink because although she was
used to admiration, it wasn't usually quite so direct.
She said repressively: 'I hope you're feeling more

comfortable, Doctor,' put a hand behind her and started to turn the door handle. 'I'll come back later—or tomorrow. . .'

'Don't go on my account,' said the large man with lazy good humour, and his voice was the voice of the man who had spoken to her on the telephone. 'When Laurens remembers I daresay he'll introduce us, although I believe there to be no need—Miss Potts, is it not? I'm the patient's cousin, Gijs van Amstel.'

He smiled gently and engulfed her hand in his large one.

'How do you do?' Serena wanted to know politely, and remembering, added: 'Why did you say incredible?'

'Ah, yes—so I did. You see, your voice isn't the kind of voice I would associate with someone called Miss Potts.'

'He's right,' said his cousin. 'What is your name? And you had better tell me or I shall call you my beautiful gipsy and cause gossip.'

Serena choked; very much on her dignity, she said: 'Potts is a good old English name,' and before any one could take her up on it, went on rapidly: 'I only came. . .I didn't know you had a visitor. . .I must be going.'

'All right, Gipsy Potts,' the young man in the bed was laughing at her, but very nicely, 'but I haven't got a visitor, only Gijs, and he doesn't count—he's come over to bail me out and get a solicitor and see about the car.'

For someone who didn't count it seemed quite a tall order; perhaps he was a poor relation or a junior partner. She took a lightning look at the man standing on the other side of the bed. He was good-

looking, she admitted rather grudgingly, if one
should fancy a high-bridged nose and a determined
chin, and although his tweed suit was superbly cut
and of good cloth, it was decidedly shabby. He
looked—she wasn't sure of the right word, for lazy
wasn't quite right, perhaps placid was the better
word, although she had once or twice detected
hidden amusement behind the placidity. She wasn't
sure if she liked him—besides, he had been beastly
about his poor injured cousin.

The poor injured cousin continued: 'I shan't be
in bed long, you know. As soon as I can get a good
stout stick in my hand, the stitches out of my head
and this damned headache gone, we'll go out and
live it up.' He looked beseechingly at her. 'You
will, won't you? And don't look like that—do say
you will.'

She found herself smiling at him because she
wanted to see him again quite badly; besides, he had
the kind of smile to charm any woman. She answered
carefully. 'Well, we'll see how you go on, shall we,
Doctor van Amstel?' and looked away to encounter
the surprisingly sharp stare of his cousin. His placid
expression hadn't altered at all; all the same, she
had the strong impression that he had been waiting
to hear what she would say.

'Call me Laurens,' commanded the younger
Doctor van Amstel.

Serena looked down at his still pale face on the
pillow. 'I'm going now,' she stated in her pleasant
voice. 'I hope you have a good night.'

She went round the bed and shook the hand the
older man was offering.

'I hope you don't have too much trouble getting
things sorted out,' she remarked, and thanked him

politely as he went to the door and opened it for her.

She met Joan outside in the corridor. Joan was tall and slim and blonde and they were firm friends. She grinned engagingly when she saw Serena and said with a chuckle: 'Stealing a march on me, ducky? I know you saw him first. . .'

'I only came up to see how he was—I didn't know he'd got someone with him—some cousin or other. . .'

'Yes, rather nice, I thought, though I've only said hullo so far. A bit sleepy, I thought.'

Serena nodded. 'Yes, I thought so too. He's come over to see to everything—I suppose he's a partner or something. I saw him downstairs, he's got the most awful old Mini,' she paused, feeling a little sorry for anyone forced to drive around in anything so battered. 'Perhaps he's not very successful.'

'Can't say the same for the patient,' said Joan. 'I hear it's an E-type Jag he was driving and it's a write-off.' She sighed. 'I don't suppose he'll be here long, though. It's a simple fracture, once he's got his walking iron on and his head's cleared, he'll be up and away.' She gave Serena a shrewd glance. 'You like him, Serena?'

'I don't know—I don't know him, do I? But he's so alive, isn't he?' she appealed to her friend, who nodded understandingly; they had both dealt with so many patients who were just the reverse.

Serena went over to the Nurses' Home and washed her smalls and then her hair, went to supper and so, presently, to bed, feeling that the evening had somehow been wasted. It would have been nice to have gone out with someone—someone like Doctor van Amstel, who would probably have been ridiculously and untruthfully flattering and made her feel like a million dollars. She went over to her mirror and stared into it; she was almost twenty-five, an old maid, she told herself, although she had probably had more proposals than any other girl in the hospital. But she had accepted none of them, for none of them had come from a man she could love. She sighed at the pretty face in the mirror and thought, a little forlornly, that perhaps she would never fall in love—really in love, especially as she wasn't quite sure what sort of a man she wanted to fall in love with. She amended that though; he might possibly look a little like the owner of the E-type Jag.

She wasn't on duty until one o'clock the next day; she got up early, made tea and toast in the little kitchen at the end of the corridor, and went out, to take a bus to Marks and Spencers in Oxford Street and browse around looking for a birthday present for her mother, who, even though she was fifty, liked pretty things. Serena settled on a pink quilted dressing gown and then loitered round the store until she barely had the time to get back to Queen's. She went on duty with seconds to spare and found the department, for once, empty, but not for long; within half an hour there was a multiple crash in, as well as an old lady who had had a coronary in the street and a small boy who had fallen off a wall on to his head. It was almost five o'clock before she could stop for a quick cup of tea in the office and it was while she was gulping it down that Joan telephoned.

'When are you off duty?' she asked. 'I've got this mad Dutchman wanting to know when you can come and see him.'

'I'm up to my eyes,' said Serena, crossly, 'and likely to be for hours yet. I'm not off until nine o'clock anyway and I doubt if I get to supper at the rate we're going.'

'Come on up when you're off, then—he needs cheering up. That cousin's been in and I don't know what he said, but Laurens is a bit down in the mouth.'

'Laurens already!' thought Serena as she said: 'Surely he wouldn't be so mean as to upset him after the accident. . .'

'Well, Laurens did tell me that he's done this sort of thing several times, and I suppose it's a bit of a nuisance for his cousin having to leave the practice and sort things out.'

'Probably,' commented Serena, not much caring. 'I'll come if I can get away in time.' She rang off, aware that whether she was on time or not, she would go.

He was lying in bed doing nothing when she got to his room at last. He looked pale and there was a discontented droop to his mouth which she put down to the after-effects of his accident; probably he still had a bad headache. But he brightened when he saw her and began to talk in a most amusing way about himself and his day. Of his cousin he said not a word and Serena didn't ask, content to be amused at his talk.

She saw him again the next morning during her dinner time, for she went, as she sometimes did, to Joan's office for the cup of tea they had before the start of the afternoon's work. It was, of necessity, a brief visit and as she left his room she passed Doctor Gijs van Amstel in the corridor. She wished him a good day and gave him the briefest of glances, because she had the feeling that if she did more than that he might be disposed to stop and talk to her,

and for some reason—too vague to put into words—
she didn't want to do that.

The next few days began to form a pattern drawn
around her visits to the surgical floor. She still went
out in her off duty, for she had a great number of
friends. She shopped too and went to the cinema
with Bill Travers, but the only real moment of the
days was when she tapped on the door of number
twenty-one and heard Laurens's welcoming: 'Come
in, Serena.'

She had seen no more of his cousin, and when
she mentioned it to Joan it was to discover that he
had returned to Holland and would be back again
shortly. And Laurens never spoke of him, although
he talked about everything else under the sun. Serena
listened, hardly speaking herself, wrapped in a kind
of enchantment because here, at last, was the man
she had been waiting for and who, she was beginning
to hope, had been waiting for her.

It surprised her that Joan, although she admitted
to liking Laurens very much, could find anything
wrong with him. 'He's a charmer all right,' she
agreed, 'but ducky, be your age—can't you see that
if he can chat you up so expertly, he's probably had
a lot of practice and doesn't intend to stop at you?'

Which remark made Serena so indignant that she
could hardly find the words to answer such heresy.
'He's not,' she insisted. 'He's cheerful and nice to
everyone, and why shouldn't we be friends while
he's here?'

Joan smiled. 'I daresay you're right, Serena, only
don't get that heart of yours broken, will you, before
you're sure it's worth risking it.'

She went home that evening, to spend her two
days off at the large, old-fashioned rectory where

her father and mother had lived for most of their married life.

She caught a later train than usual that evening, because she had gone to see Laurens first and it was quite dark by the time she got out at Dorchester to find her father waiting for her in the old-fashioned Rover he had had for such a long time. She kissed him with affection and got in beside him, suddenly glad at the prospect of the peace and quiet of home. They didn't talk much as they went through the town and out on to the road to Maiden Newton because she didn't want to distract her parent's attention. He was an unworldly man in many ways; he had never quite realized that traffic had increased since he had first taken to motoring; in consequence he drove with a carefree disregard for other cars which could be alarming unless, like his family, his companions knew him well.

Serena, who had iron nerves and was a passable driver herself, suffered the journey calmly enough; there wasn't a great deal of traffic on the road and once through Frampton they turned off into a winding lane which although narrow, held no terrors for either of them for they knew every yard of it.

The village, when they reached it at the bottom of a steep hill, was already in darkness; only the Rectory's old-fashioned wide windows sent splashes of brightness into the lane as they turned in the always open gate. They had barely stopped before the door was flung open, and Serena jumped out to meet her family.

CHAPTER TWO

THERE were quite a lot of people in the doorway—
her mother, as small as Serena herself and almost
as slim, Susan, who was seventeen and constantly
in the throes of some affair of the heart, so that
everyone else had the utmost difficulty in remembering the name of the current boyfriend, Margery,
twenty, and married only a few months earlier to
her father's curate, a situation which afforded great
pleasure to the family and her mother, especially
because she was the plain one of the children, and
Serena's two young brothers, home from boarding
school for the Easter holidays—Dan was twelve and
George, the youngest, was ten. Their father hoped
that they would follow in his footsteps and go into
the Church, and probably they would, but in the
meantime they got up to all the tricks boys of their
age usually indulged in.

It was lovely to be home again; she was swept
inside on a cheerful tide of greetings and family
news, all of which would have to be repeated later
on, but in the meantime the cheerful babble of talk
was very pleasant. 'Where's John?' Serena tossed
her hat on to the nearest chair and addressed
Margery.

'He'll be here. He had to go and see old Mrs
Spike, you know—down by Buller's Meadow, she's
hurt her leg and can't get about.'

Serena took off her coat and sent it to join her

hat. 'Being married suits you, Margery—you're all glowing.'

Her sister smiled. 'Well, that's how it makes you feel. How's the hospital?'

'Oh, up and down, you know. . .it's nice to get away.'

They smiled at each other as Serena flung an arm around her mother's shoulders and asked her how she was. The rest of the evening passed in a pleasurable exchange of news and the consuming of the supper Mrs Potts had prepared. They all sat around the too large mahogany table, talking and eating and laughing a great deal. The dining-room was faintly mid-Victorian and gloomy with it, but they were all so familiar with it that no one noticed its drawbacks. Presently, when there was no more to be eaten and they had talked themselves to a standstill, they washed up and went back to the sitting-room, to talk again until midnight and later, when they parted for the night and Serena went to her old room at the back of the house, to lie in her narrow bed and wonder what Laurens van Amstel was doing.

Breakfast was half over the next morning when the telephone rang; no one took any notice of it— no one, that was, but Susan, for the family had come to learn during the last few months that almost all the telephone calls were for her, and rather than waste time identifying the young man at the other end of the line, finding Susan and then returning to whatever it was they had been interrupted in doing, it was far better for all concerned if she answered all the calls herself. She tore away now, saying over her shoulder: 'That'll be Bert,' and Serena looked up from her plate to exclaim: 'But it was Gavin last time I was home—what happened to him?'

Her mother looked up from her letters. 'Gavin?' She looked vague. 'I believe he went to. . .'

She was interrupted by Susan. 'It's for you,' she told Serena. 'A man.'

Serena rose without haste, avoiding the eyes focused upon her. 'Some query at the hospital,' she suggested airily as she walked, not too fast, out of the room, aware that if that was all it was, she was going to be disappointed. There was no reason why Laurens should telephone—he didn't even know where she was; all the same she hoped that it was he.

She went into her father's study and picked up the receiver. Her voice didn't betray her excitement as she said: 'Hullo?'

It was Laurens; his voice came gaily over the wire. 'Serena!'

'How did you know where I was?' She sounded, despite her efforts, breathless.

He laughed softly. 'Your friend Joan—such a nice girl—after all, there's no reason why I shouldn't know where you live, is there? What are you doing?'

'Having breakfast. I'm not sure that I. . .'

'You're not sure about anything, are you, my dear gipsy? I miss you. When are you coming back?'

'On Monday. I come up on an early morning train.'

'Not this time—I'll send Gijs down to pick you up, he'll drive you.'

She shook her head, although he wasn't there to see her vehement refusal.

'No, thank you, I prefer to go by train—it's very kind. . .'

'Rubbish! Gijs won't mind, he does anything any-one asks of him—more fool he.' He spoke jokingly and she laughed with him.

'All the same, I'd rather come up by train.'

He sounded very persuasive. 'Not to please me? I hate to think of you travelling in a crowded train, and at least Gijs can give you lunch.'

She said in a panicky little voice: 'But that's impossible. I'm on duty at one o'clock.'

'My beautiful gipsy, how difficult you make everything! Gijs will pick you up about nine o'clock on Monday morning. What are you going to do today?'

'Nothing very interesting, just—just be at home.' How could she tell him that she was going to make the beds for her mother and probably get the lunch ready as well and spend the afternoon visiting the sexton's wife who had just had another baby, and the organist's wife, who'd just lost hers? She felt relief when he commented casually: 'It sounds nice. Come and see me on Monday, Serena.'

'Yes—at least, I will if I can get away. You know how it is.'

'Indeed I do—the quicker you leave it the better.'

'Leave it?' she repeated his words faintly.

'Of course—had you not thought of marrying me?'

Serena was bereft of words. 'I—I—' she began, and then: 'I must go,' she managed at last. 'Goodbye.'

'Goodbye, gipsy girl, I shall see you on Monday.'

She nodded foolishly without speaking and replaced the receiver gently. She hadn't heard aright, of course, and even if she had, he must have been joking—he joked a lot. She sat down in her father's chair behind his desk, quite forgetful of breakfast, trying to sort out her feelings. They slid silkily in and out of her head, evading her efforts to pin them down—the only thought which remained clearly and firmly in her mind was the one concerning Gijs van Amstel; she didn't want to go back to London with him. The idea of being in his company for several hours disquieted her, although she didn't know why; he had done nothing to offend or annoy her, indeed, he had exerted himself to be civil, and she had no interest in him, only the fact that he was Laurens's cousin was the common denominator of their acquaintance, so, she told herself vigorously, she was merely being foolish.

She went back to her interrupted breakfast then, and although no one asked her any questions at all she felt compelled to explain into the eloquent silence. When she had finished, omitting a great deal, her mother remarked: 'He sounds nice, dear, such a change from your usual patients—is his English good?'

Serena, grateful for her parent's tactful help, told her that yes, it was, very good.

'And this cousin—he's coming to fetch you on Monday morning?'

Serena drank her cold tea. 'Yes.'

'Where will he sleep?' her mother, a practical woman, wanted to know.

Serena's lovely eyes opened wide. She hadn't given a thought to the man who was coming to fetch her, and now, upon thinking about it, she really didn't care where he slept. Perhaps he would leave early in the morning. She suggested this light-heartedly and her mother mused: 'He must be a very nice man then, to spoil a night's sleep to come and collect someone he doesn't even know well.'

'Oh,' said Serena, her head full of Laurens, 'he seems to do exactly what Laurens tells him—I suppose he's a poor relation or a junior partner or something of that sort. He's got the most awful old car.'

'Oh?' it was her father this time. 'Is he a very young man, then?'

Serena dragged her thoughts away from Laurens and considered. 'Oh, no—he must be years older—he looks about thirty-five, I suppose. I haven't really noticed.'

Her mother gave her a swift, penetrating glance and said with deceptive casualness: 'Well, we can find out on Monday, can't we?' she smiled at her eldest child. 'And how old is this Laurence?'

'Laurens,' Serena corrected her gently. 'About twenty-six.'

'Good-looking?' asked Susan, who had been sitting silent all this time, not saying a word.

'Yes, very. Fair and tall.'

'What a rotten description,' Susan sounded faintly bored. 'If you've finished, shall we get washed up? There's such a lot to do and there's never time.'

Serena rose obediently from the table, understanding very well that what her younger sister meant was not enough time to do her hair a dozen ways before settling on the day's style, nor time enough to see to her nails, or try out a variety of lipsticks. She sighed unconsciously, remembering how nice it was to be seventeen and fall painlessly in and out of love and pore for hours over magazines—she felt suddenly rather old.

In the end she did the washing up herself because Susan had her telephone call and the two boys disappeared with the completeness and silence which only boys achieve. She stood at the old-fashioned kitchen sink and as she worked she thought about

Laurens, trying to make herself think sensibly. No one in their right minds fell in love like this, to the exclusion of everything and everyone else. She was, she reminded herself over and over again, a sensible girl, no longer young and silly like little Susan; she saw also that, there was a lot more to marriage than falling in love. Besides, Laurens, even though he had told her so delightfully and surprisingly that she was going to marry him—for surely that was what he had meant—might be in the habit of falling in love with any girl who chanced to take his fancy. She began to dry the dishes, resolving that, whatever her feelings, she would not allow herself to be hurried into any situation, however wonderful it might seem. She had put the china and silver away and was on her way upstairs to make the beds when she remembered the strange intent look Gijs van Amstel had given her when Laurens had suggested she should go out with him. There had been no reason for it and it puzzled her that the small episode should stick so firmly in her memory. She shook it free from her thoughts and joined her mother, already busy in the boys' room.

The day passed pleasantly so that she forgot her impatience for Monday's arrival. When she had finished her chores she duly visited the sexton's wife, admired the baby—the sixth and surely the last?—presented the proud mother with a small gift for the tiny creature, and turned her attention to the sexton's other five children, who had arrived with an almost monotonous regularity every eighteen months or so. They all bore a marked resemblance to each other and, Serena had to admit, they all looked remarkably healthy. She asked tentatively: 'Do you find it a bit much—six, Mrs Snow?'

Her hostess smiled broadly. 'Lor' no, Miss Serena, they'm good as gold and proper little loves, we wouldn't be without 'em. You'll see, when you'm wed and 'as little 'uns to rear.'

Serena tried to imagine herself with six small children, and somehow the picture was blurred because deep in her bones something told her that Laurens wouldn't want to be bothered with a houseful of children to absorb her time—and his. He would want her for himself... The thought sent a small doubt niggling at the back of her mind, for she loved children; provided she had help she was quite sure she could cope with half a dozen, but only if their father did his share too, and Laurens, she was sure, even though she knew very little about him, wasn't that kind of man. Disconcertingly, a picture of his cousin, lolling against the bed in his well-worn tweeds, crossed her thoughts; she had no doubt that he would make an excellent father, even though he did strike her as being a thought too languid in his manner. And probably he was already a parent. He was, after all, older than Laurens and must have settled down by now. She dismissed him from her mind, bade the happy mother and her offspring goodbye, and departed to make her second visit—a more difficult one—the organist's wife had lost a small baby since Serena had been home last, it had been a puny little creature with a heart condition which everyone knew was never going to improve, but that hadn't made it any easier for the mother. Serena spent longer there than she had meant to do, trying to comfort the poor woman while she reflected how unfair life could be.

It was surprising how quickly the weekend flew by, and yet, looking back on it as she dressed on the Monday morning, Serena saw that it had been a tranquil, slow-moving period, with time to do everything at leisure. As she made up her pretty face she found herself wishing that she wasn't going back to Queen's, to the eternal bustle and rush of the Accident Room, the hurried meals and the off duty, when one was either too tired to do anything but fall into one's bed, or possessed of the feverish urge to rush out and enjoy oneself. But if she didn't go back she wouldn't see Laurens. She tucked back a stray wisp of hair and stood back to inspect her person; she was wearing a short-sleeved silk blouse which exactly matched the deep clotted cream of her pleated skirt, whose matching jacket she left on the bed with her gloves and handbag, for she still had the breakfast to get. She put on the kettle, skipped into the dining-room and tuned the radio in to the music programme and went back to the stove, trying out a few dance steps to the too-loud music as she cracked eggs into a bowl. She dropped the last one on to the floor when a voice behind her said almost apologetically: 'I must take the blame for that, but the front door was open and although I rang the bell the music—er—drowned it, I fancy.'

She had whirled round and trodden in the egg as she did so. She said:

'Damn!' and then: 'Good morning, Doctor van Amstel, you're early,' giving him the briefest of smiles.

If he was put out by his cool reception he allowed nothing of it to show but said mildly: 'Yes, I'm sorry for that, too, but Laurens was so anxious that I should be on time.' His unhurried gaze took in the apron she had tied untidily round her slim waist and moved on to take in the singing kettle and the bacon sizzling in the pan. 'I'll come back in half an hour, shall I?' He gave her a lazy grin and sauntered towards the door just as Mrs Potts trotted in. Showing no surprise at the sight of a very large strange man in her kitchen, she said briskly: 'Good morning. You'll be the cousin, I'm sure. How very early you must have got up this morning, you poor boy. You'll have breakfast with us, of course, it'll be ready in a minute.'

Serena dished up bacon and put another few slices in. She felt all at once exasperated; she had been rude and inhospitable and the poor man had presumably had no breakfast; after all, he was driving her back. She said contritely: 'I'm so sorry—I was surprised—I think I must have lost my wits. This is Doctor Gijs van Amstel, Mother—my mother, Doctor, and this is my father,' she added as her parent joined them. She left them to talk while she got on with the toast, peeping once or twice at the doctor. He dwarfed her father both in height and breadth, his massive head with its pale hair towering over them all. He appeared to be getting on very well with her mother and father and something about his manner made her wonder if her first impression of him had been wrong—perhaps he wasn't a junior partner at all. Her arched brows drew together in a frown as she pondered this; there was so much she didn't know about Laurens and this man standing beside her.

They left directly after breakfast, with the entire family waving goodbye from the door and an odd housewife or so from the nearby cottages waving too for good measure. The car bumped a little going up the lane and the doctor said easily: 'Sorry about the car—I really must do something about it.' He slowed a little as they turned into the wider road.

'But I must get Laurens settled first. His car's a write-off, I'm afraid.'

'Was it his fault?'

He didn't look at her. 'Yes, but I believe his solicitor may be able to prove mitigating circumstances.' Something in his voice caused Serena to keep silent, but when he went on: 'Laurens has already ordered a new car,' she exclaimed: 'Another E-type Jag?'

'Yes—a car with great pulling power, I have discovered—especially where girls are concerned.'

Serena's lovely face was washed with a rich pink. 'What an offensive remark!' she uttered in an arctic voice. 'Just because you've got an old Mini. . .' she stopped, aware that she was being even more offensive.

'With no pulling power at all?' he was laughing at her. 'Too true, Miss Potts,' and then to surprise her, 'I wonder why you dislike me?'

'Disl. . .' Serena, not usually flustered, was. 'I don't—that is, I don't know you—how could I possibly. . . I've no idea what you're talking about.'

'No? Have you read Samuel Butler?'

'No—not to remember. A poet, wasn't he—seventeenth century. Why?'

' "Quoth Hudibras, I smell a rat; Ralpho, thou dost prevaricate." '

The pink, which had subsided nicely, returned. 'I'm not prevaricating—well, perhaps, a little.'

'That's better. I always feel that one can't be friends with anyone until one has achieved honesty.'

She asked, bewildered: 'Are we to be friends?'

'We're bound to see quite a lot of each other, are we not? I think we might make the effort—I'm quite harmless, you know.'

She wondered if he was; his manner was casual

and he talked with an air of not minding very much about anything—on the other hand, he read an early English poet well enough to quote him. She inquired: 'Where did you learn to speak such good English?'

They were going slowly through Dorchester, caught up in the early morning traffic. He shrugged. 'Oh, I don't know—school, and visits here, and university.'

'A Dutch university?'

'Yes.' And that was all he said, much to her annoyance; for all his casual air he was hardly forthcoming. Never one to give up, she tried again. 'Do you know this part of England well?'

'Moderately well. I came here when I was a boy.' His lips twitched with amusement, he added: 'Visiting, you know.'

She didn't know, which was so annoying, but she gave up after that and sat in silence while he urged the little car along the road to Puddletown and beyond to Wimborne. They were approaching that small town when he observed; 'You're very quiet.'

There were a number of tart replies she would have liked to make to that, but instead she said meekly: 'I thought perhaps you liked to drive without talking—some people do.'

'My dear good girl, did I give you that impression? You must forgive me—let us by all means talk.' Which he proceeded to do, very entertainingly, as he sent the Mini belting along towards the Winchester bypass. Going through Farnham he said: 'I haven't stopped for coffee—I thought that a little nearer London would serve our purpose better. You're on duty at one o'clock, I gather.'

She admitted that she was. 'It was kind of you to

come,' she began. 'It's taken up a great deal of your day.'

'Well, I can't think of a better way of spending it,' he replied pleasantly. 'I don't much care for London—a day or so is all right, but it's hardly my cup of tea.'

'Oh? What's your cup of tea, Doctor?'

'A small town, I suppose, where I know everyone and everyone knows me, a good day's work and a shelf full of good books and German to keep me company.'

She was aware of an odd sensation which she didn't stop to pursue. 'Your wife?'

His bellow of laughter rocked the car. 'My dog— a dachshund and a bossy little beast. He goes everywhere with me.'

'He must miss you.'

'Yes, but Jaap and his wife, who live with me, take good care of him.'

She tried to envisage his home. Did he live in digs? It sounded like it, but surely he had a surgery— or did he share Laurens's? She longed to ask but decided against it. Instead she started to talk about the hospital, a topic which seemed safe ground and devoid of conversational pitfalls.

It was almost midday when he turned off the A30 and took the road to Hampton where he pulled up outside the Greyhound. 'Ten minutes?' he suggested. 'Just time for something quick—it will have to be sandwiches, I'm afraid, too bad we couldn't have made it lunch.'

Serena murmured a polite nothing because her mind was so full of seeing Laurens again that even ten minutes' stop was irksome. She drank the coffee he ordered and nibbled at a selection of sandwiches with concealed impatience.

She had exactly fifteen minutes to change when they reached Queen's. She thanked her companion hurriedly, said that she supposed that she would see him again, and fled to the Nurses' Home, to emerge ten minutes later as neat as a new pin and not a hair out of place. She was, in fact, one minute early on duty—and a good thing too, she decided as she made her way through the trolleys, ambulance men, nurses and patients and fetched up by Betsy, who said at once: 'Oh, good! Thank heaven you're here. I'm fed up, I can tell you—not a moment's peace the whole morning. There's a cardiac arrest in the first cubicle, an overdose in the second and an old lady who slipped on a banana skin—she's got an impacted fracture of neck of femur—oh, and there's an RTA on the way in—two so far, both conscious and a third I don't even know about yet.'

'Charming,' declared Serena, 'and I suppose no one's been to dinner.'

'Oh, yes, they have—Harris. Yes, I knew you'd be pleased, ducky, but take heart, you've got your two part-timers coming on in half an hour. Harris can't do much harm in that time.'

'You must be joking, Betsy. Thanks for holding the fort, anyway. See you later.' Serena was taking off her cuffs and rolling up her sleeves ready for work. She cast her eyes upwards, adding: 'If I survive.'

She paused at about four o'clock when the immediate emergencies had been dealt with and the part-time staff nurses, back from their tea, took over. In the office she accepted the tea Agnes had made for her and started to sort out the papers on her desk.

It was amazing that so much could accumulate in two days. She was half way through a long-winded direction as to the disposal of plastic syringes and their needles when the telephone rang. It was Joan, wanting to know impatiently why she hadn't been up to see Laurens.

'You must be out of your tiny mind,' said Serena crossly. 'I haven't sat down since I got back until this very minute and if I get up there this evening, it'll be a miracle.'

She slammed down the receiver, feeling mean, and knowing that her ill-humour was partly because she hadn't been able to get up to Surgical, and saw no chance of doing so until she went off duty that evening. She would apologize to Joan when she saw her. She poured herself another cup of tea and went back to the disposable plastic syringes.

It was gone half past nine when Serena at last went off duty. The night staff nurse and her companion, a male nurse, because sometimes things got a bit rough at night, had come on punctually, but there had been clearing up to do and Serena had elected to send the day duty nurses off and stay to clear up the mess herself. She had missed supper and she thought longingly of a large pot of tea and a piled-high plate of toast as she wended her way through the hospital towards Surgical. One of the Night Sisters was already there because it had been theatre day and there were several post-op. cases needing a watchful eye. She said 'Hullo,' to Serena when she saw her and added: 'He's still awake, do go in.'

Serena, tapping on the door of number twenty-one, wondered if the whole hospital knew about her friendship with the Dutch doctor and dismissed the idea with a shrug. He was in bed, although he told

her immediately in something like triumph that he
was to have a walking iron fixed the following morning and that his concussion had cleared completely.
'Come here, my little gipsy,' he cajoled her. 'I've
been so bored all day, I thought you were never
coming.'

'I told Joan. . .' she began.

'Yes, I know—surely you could have left one of
your nurses in charge for just a moment or two? I
was furious with Gijs getting back so late—if he'd
moved a bit you would have had time to come and
see me before you went on duty.'

'He did move,' said Serena soothingly. 'I've never
seen anyone get so much out of a middle-aged Mini
in all my life. He was very kind, too. . .'

'Oh, Gijs is always kind.' Laurens sounded a little
sulky and she gave him a startled look which made
him change the sulkiness for a smile of great charm.
'Sorry I'm so foul-tempered—it's a bit dull, you
know. Come a little nearer, I shan't bite.'

She went and stood close to the bed and he
reached up and pulled her down and kissed her
swiftly. 'There,' he said with satisfaction, 'now
everything's fine—no, don't go away.'

She smiled a little shyly and left her hand in his,
studying his good looks—he really was remarkably
handsome. It was strange that all unbidden, the face
of his cousin should float before her eyes—he was
handsome too, but with a difference which she didn't
bother to discover just then, although it reminded her
to ask: 'Your cousin—I hope he wasn't too tired?'

'Gijs? Tired? Lord no, he's never tired. He went
back to Holland this evening.'

Serena felt a faint prick of disappointment; she
hadn't thanked him properly and now she might

never have the opportunity. She said so worriedly and Laurens laughed. 'Don't give it a thought, he wouldn't expect it. And now let's stop talking about Gijs and talk about us.'

'Us?'

He nodded. 'I'll be fit to get around in a couple of days—I shan't be able to drive or dance, but there's no reason why we shouldn't have dinner together, is there, Serena? When are you free in the evening?'

She told him and he went on. 'Good—I should get away from here by Thursday or Friday. We'll dine and make plans.'

Serena, conscious that her conversation, such as it was, had become repetitive, asked 'Plans?'

'Of course, my beauty—there's our glorious future to discuss.'

Serena forced herself to remain calm. All the same, he was going a bit fast for her; perhaps she should change the conversation. She asked sedately: 'When will you go back to Holland?' wisely not commenting upon the future.

He smiled a little as though he knew what she was thinking. 'We'll talk about that later. Quite soon, I expect—my mother is worrying about me. She's a splendid worrier, though Gijs will be home by the morning and can soothe her down—he's good at that. If ever you want a good cry, Serena, try his shoulder. He's splendid in the part—doesn't seem to mind a girl crying, though I can't say the same for myself. I've not much patience for women who burst into tears for no good reason.'

He grinned at her and she smiled back, thinking how absurd it was for anyone to want to cry about anything at all. 'I'm going,' she said softly. 'Night

Sister will hate me if I stay a moment longer.' She withdrew her hand.

'Come tomorrow,' he urged her as she reached the door. She turned to look at him and even at that distance, in the light of the bedside lamp, she could see how blue his eyes were. 'Of course.'

On the way over to the home she found herself wondering what colour Gijs's eyes were. It was ridiculous, but she didn't know; blue too, she supposed, and now she came to think about it, he had a habit of drooping the lids which was probably why she didn't know. In any case, it was quite unimportant.

Laurens went on Thursday, but not before he had arranged to see Serena on Friday evening. 'I'll be at the Stafford, in St James' Place,' he had told her. 'I'll send a taxi for you—seven o'clock, if that's OK.'

She had agreed, enchanted that she was to see him again so soon. She had visited him every day and they had laughed a lot together, and he had been gay and charming and had made no secret of the fact that he was more than a little in love with her, and even though she still felt a little uncertain as to his true feelings she had allowed herself to dwell on a future which excited her.

For once, and to her great relief, she was off duty punctually so that she had time to bath and dress with care in a dress the colour of corn. It was very plain and she covered it with a matching wool coat; the only ornament she wore was an old-fashioned keeper ring her father had given her on her twenty-first birthday which had belonged to her great-grandmother.

The hotel was small as London hotels went, but entering its foyer, she suspected that it catered for people who enjoyed the comforts of life and were prepared to pay for them. She hadn't thought much about Laurens's state as regards money. He had an E-type Jaguar, certainly, but a great many young men had those, affording them at the expense of something else, but it seemed that he could afford his Jag and a good life too. She inquired for him with pleasant composure and was relieved of her coat and ushered into the hotel lounge. He was waiting for her, looking very correct in his black tie, although she found his shirt over-fussy. Even as she smiled in greeting her eyes swept down to his leg and he laughed. 'Serena, forget your wretched plasters for an hour or two—it's quite safe inside my trouser. I got one of the fellows to cut the seam and pin it together again.'

She laughed then. 'How frightfully wasteful! Are you all right here—comfortable?'

A silly remark, she chided herself, but she hadn't been able to think of anything else to say in her delight at seeing him.

'Very comfortable,' he told her, 'and now you're here, perfectly all right.' He smiled at her. 'Will a Dubonnet suit you, or would you rather have a gin and lime?'

'Dubonnet, thank you. When are you going home?'

'On Saturday—Gijs will come over for me. I'll be back in a few weeks, though, to collect the new car.' His hand covered hers briefly where it lay on the table. 'Serena, will you come over to Holland—oh, not now—in a few weeks. I want you to meet my mother.'

She blinked her long lashes, her eyes enormous with surprise. 'But why—I haven't any holiday due.'

'Who spoke of holidays? You can resign or what-ever it is you do, can't you?'

'But I shall want to go back. . .'

'Now that's something we're going to talk about.' He smiled as he spoke and her own mouth curved in response.

She ate her dinner in a happy daze, saying very little, not quite sure that it was really all happening, until he asked suddenly: 'Why do you wear that ring? It's a cheap thing. I'll give you a ring to suit your beautiful finger—diamonds, I think.'

Serena felt affronted and a little hurt, but all the same she explained without showing it that it was her great-grandmother's and that she treasured it. 'And I don't like diamonds,' she added quietly.

Her words had the effect of amusing him very much. 'My sweet gipsy, you can't mean that—all girls like diamonds.'

Serena took a mouthful of crême brulée and said, smiling a little, because it was impossible to be even faintly annoyed with him: 'Well, here's one girl who doesn't.'

'And that's something else we'll talk about later,' he said lightly. 'When are you free tomorrow?'

She told him happily. 'And Saturday?' She told him that too. 'I'm on at ten for the rest of the day.'

'Good lord, why?'

She explained about weekends and was gratify-ingly flattered when he observed: 'Just my luck— if it had been last weekend, we could have spent it together.'

'Not very well,' Serena, being a parson's daugh-ter, saw no hidden meanings in this remark, 'for you can't drive and I haven't got a car, you know, and the train journey would have tired you out.'

She spoke happily because it had made everything seem more real because he had taken it for granted that he would have spent the weekend at her home. She certainly didn't notice the hastily suppressed astonishment in his voice when he answered her.

They talked about other things then, and it was only when she was wishing him goodbye, with the promise to lunch with him on the next day, that he said:

'You're quite a girl, Serena—full of surprises, too.' He kissed her lightly on the cheek and added: 'Tomorrow.'

She went to bed in a haze of dreams, all of them with happy endings, and none of them, she realized when she woke in the morning, capable of standing up to a searching scrutiny. She decided rebelliously that she wasn't going to be searching anyway. She dressed with care in the white jacket and skirt and decided against a hat.

They had almost finished their early lunch when Laurens said: 'I shan't see you tomorrow then, my sweet. I shall miss you—will you miss me?'

Serena had never been encouraged to be anything but honest. 'Yes, of course,' she answered readily 'very much. But you're coming back—you said. . .'

He laughed a little. 'Oh, yes, I'm coming back, and next time when I go you're coming with me, remember?'

'Well, yes,' she stammered a little, 'but I wasn't sure if you meant it.'

He put his head on one side. 'Then you must be sure. I shall ring you up when I get back, then you will give in your notice to your so good Matron and pack your bags and come to my home and learn something of Holland.'

'Oh,' said Serena, her heart was pattering along at a great rate, 'are you—that is, is this. . .'

'It seems so. How else am I to get you, my beautiful gipsy?'

They said goodbye soon after that and when he kissed her she returned his kiss with a happy warmth even though she couldn't bear the thought of not seeing him for several weeks.

It was fortunate that when she got on duty there was a dearth of patients; it hadn't been so quiet for weeks. Serena sat in her office, making out the off duty and requisition forms and holiday lists and all the while her head spun with a delightful dreamlike speed, littered with a host of ideas, all of which she was far too excited to go into. It was like dipping into a box of unexpected treasure, and some of her happiness showed on her face so that her friends, noticing it, exchanged meaningful glances amongst themselves.

She had thought that she wouldn't sleep that night, but she did, and dreamlessly too, and she was glad to have had a good night's rest when she went on duty in the morning, for the Accident Room was going at full pressure. About half past eleven there was a lull, however, so she went along to her office and drank her coffee and thought about Laurens; she had forgotten to ask him at what time he was going; perhaps he was already on his way. . . The wistful thought was interrupted by one of the nurses with the news that there was a flasher coming in.

Only one ambulance man came in, carrying a very small bundle in a blanket. As soon as he saw her he said, 'Glad you're on, Sister. I got a battered baby here. Proper knocked about, she is. . .'

Serena forget all about Laurens then. She whisked

into the nearest cubicle, saying: 'Here, Jones, any idea what happened?' She was already unwrapping the blanket from the small stiff form and winced when she saw the little bruised body. Without pausing in her task she said: 'Nurse, telephone Mr Travers, please—he's on duty, isn't he? Ask him to come at once—tell him it's a battered baby.'

She had her scissors out now and was cutting the odds and ends of grubby clothing from the baby's body. 'Well, Jones?'

'Neighbours,' he began. 'They heard a bit of a bust-up like, and went to fetch the police—the coppers took the baby's dad off with them, the mum too. There'll be a copper round to inquire. Hit her with a belt, they said.'

'With a buckle on the end of it, Jones. The brute—I'd like to get my hands on him!' Which, considering she was five foot three and small with it, was an absurd thing to say, although the ambulance man knew what she meant.

'Me, too,' he said soberly. 'Shall I give the particulars to nurse, Sister?'

'Yes, please.' She was sponging, with infinite care, the abrasions and cuts, hoping she would be able to complete the cleaning process before the baby became conscious again.

Bill was beside her and as she wiped the last of the superficial dirt away, bent over the baby. 'Alive, anyway,' he observed, and spoke to someone behind her—someone she hadn't known was there and who came round to the other side of the examination table as Bill spoke. Doctor Gijs van Amstel. 'You don't mind, Serena,' Bill was intent on the baby, 'if Doctor van Amstel has a look? He's by way of being an authority on this sort of thing and he happened to be here. . .'

Serena nodded, staring at the calm face of the man opposite her, and then went a bright pink because if he was here, surely Laurens would be with him. She dismissed the idea at once because it was hardly the time to let her thoughts stray. She watched the large, quiet man bend over the baby in his turn. His hands were very gentle despite their size, and although there was no expression on his face she knew that he was angry. He said nothing at all until he had finished his examination. Then: 'I find the same as you Bill—concussion, suspected ruptured spleen—you felt that? and I wonder what fractures we shall see. . .this arm, I fancy, and these fourth and fifth ribs, there could possibly be a greenstick fracture of this left leg—you agree?'

Bill Travers nodded and Serena found herself admiring the Dutchman for fielding the diagnosis back to the younger, less experienced man. She gave Bill the X-ray form she had ready and then sent a nurse speeding ahead with it, and when she prepared to take the baby she found that both men were with her. The Dutchman seemed to know the radiologist too—the three men crowded into the dark room to study the still wet films and when they came out it was the radiologist who spoke. 'A couple of green-stick fractures of the left humerus, a hairline fracture of the left femur, and a crack in the temporal bone—and of course the spleen. Quite shocking. . .have the police got the man who did it?'

'Yes,' said Serena savagely, 'they have, and I hope they put him in prison for life.' She signed to the nurse who had come with her and they wheeled the trolley back to the Accident Room and presently the men joined her.

'I've telephoned the boss,' Bill told her—the boss was Mr Sedgley, tall and thin and stooping and wonderful with children. 'She's to go straight to theatre. OK, Serena?'

She was drawing a loose gown over the puny frame. She nodded and arranged a small blanket over the gown, then wrote out the baby's identity on the plastic bracelet she slipped on its wrist. Which done, she sent for the porters and leaving the nurse in charge, went with the baby straight to theatre.

When she got back Bill was still there, so was Doctor van Amstel. There was a policeman with them too and Serena lifted her eyebrows at one of the student nurses, who disappeared, to appear with commendable speed carrying a tray of tea. 'You too, Sister?' she whispered. But Serena shook her head; she couldn't drink tea until she had got the taste of the battered baby out of her mouth. She left the nurses to do the clearing up and went back to her office; the case would have to be entered in the day book and she still had the list of surgical requirements to tackle. She was half way through this when there was a tap on the door and Doctor van Amstel came in. He wasted no time. 'You must be wondering why I am here and if Laurens is with me. I called to settle some bills and so forth and convey his thanks—he didn't feel like coming himself. And I want to thank you for taking such good care of him and for cheering him up while he was here. He hates inaction, you know.'

She sat at her desk, looking at him and wishing he would go away. The baby had upset her—she was used to horrible and unpleasant sights, but this

one had been so pointless and so cruel, and now on
top of that this man had to come—why couldn't it
have been Laurens?

She said woodenly: 'That's quite all right. It must
have been very dull for him, but he'll soon be fit
again, won't he?'

He nodded. 'A pity,' he observed slowly, 'that
we shan't meet again.' His voice was casual, but his
eyes, under their drooping lids, were not.

'Oh, but I daresay we shall,' Serena declared.
'Laurens has asked me over to stay with his
mother—I expect we shall see each other then.' She
glanced up at him as she spoke and was surprised
to see, for a brief moment, fierce anger in his face;
it had gone again so quickly that afterwards she
decided that she had imagined it.

'Indeed?' his voice was placid. 'That will be
pleasant—when do you plan to come?'

'I—don't know. Laurens is going to telephone
or write.'

'Ah, yes, of course.' He held out a hand. 'I shall
look forward to seeing you again, Miss Potts—or
perhaps, since you are to—er—continue your
friendship with Laurens, I may call you Serena, and
you must learn to call me Gijs.'

He smiled and went to the door and then came
back again to say in quite a different voice: 'I'm
sorry about the baby. I'm angry too.'

She nodded wordlessly, knowing that he meant
what he said. He closed the door very quietly behind
him and she listened to his unhurried footsteps
retreating across the vast expanse of the Accident
Room and wondered why she felt so lonely.

CHAPTER THREE

THE days were incredibly dull; it wasn't so bad while she was on duty, for the Accident Room, whatever else it was, could hardly be called dull. But off duty was another matter, and for the first three days she heard nothing from Laurens either. It was on the fourth morning that she had a letter from him, a brief, cheerful missive which told her nothing of the things she wanted to know. She waited two days before answering it and then wrote a stilted page or so in reply, and the following day was sorry she had done so, for a reed basket full to the brim with roses arrived for her with a card inside saying: 'To my gipsy from Laurens.' She felt better after that and better still when he telephoned that evening. He sounded in tearing spirits and her own spirits soared, to erupt skyhigh when he asked:

'Will you give in your notice tomorrow, Serena?—I'll be coming over in a month's time to collect the car, and I want to bring you back with me.'

She gasped a little, then: 'You mean that, Laurens? You truly mean that?'

'My darling creature, don't be so timid. Will you do it? I don't approve of working wives, you know.'

It wasn't quite a proposal, but it was probably all she would ever get. She agreed breathlessly and was rewarded by his: 'Good girl, I'll tell you the date and so on next time I ring up. 'Bye for now.'

She replaced the receiver because he hadn't

waited for her to wish him goodbye—perhaps, she thought, he felt as excited as she was. She went up to her room, and while her common sense lay buried under a mass of excited thoughts, she wrote out her resignation.

She hadn't realized that Matron was going to be so surprised and so openly critical. She had accepted the resignation, of course; there was nothing else she could do, but she had questioned Serena's wisdom while she did so.

'You're a sensible young woman,' she told a surprised Serena, 'and certainly old enough to know what you're doing. But do you think you have given the matter enough thought?' And when Serena had nodded emphatically, went on: 'At least I will say this, if things should not turn out as you expect them to, you may rest assured that there will always be some kind of a job for you here—perhaps not in this hospital, but in one of the annexes.'

Serena had thanked her nicely, knowing that Miss Shepherd had her welfare at heart, knowing too, that nothing would persuade her to work in one of the annexes—Geriatrics, Convalescent, the dental department, Rehabilitation; she could think of nothing she disliked more, and in any case there was no need for her to think about them at all, for the likelihood of her returning to hospital was a laughable impossibility. She even smiled kindly at Miss Shepherd because the poor dear was all of forty-five and there was no wonderful young man waiting for her to be his bride, then thanked her politely and went back to her department and in due course, to the dining-room for her dinner, where her appearance, hugely enhanced by excitement and happiness, drew so many comments from her friends that she felt compelled to tell them her news, so happy in the telling that she didn't notice the worried little frown on Betsy's face nor the look she and Joan exchanged.

It was Joan who spoke after the first babble of congratulations had died down. 'Serena,' she began, 'are you sure? I mean, you don't know anything about his home or his family and you might hate Holland.'

'Well, I've thought about that, and I don't see how I'm to know unless I go there and see for myself.' She pinkened faintly. 'I mean, we—I can always change my mind.'

Joan agreed with her a little too hastily and Betsy said: 'Your parents, I bet they're surprised.'

'I haven't told them yet. I told them about Laurens coming in and—and how nice he was, and of course they met his cousin.'

'Oh, yes, I forgot. Though they're not a bit alike, are they?'

Serena spooned sugar into her post-prandial cup of tea. 'Heavens, no,' she agreed, and just for a brief moment remembered the gentle touch of Gijs van Amstel's hands on the battered baby. She had never seen Laurens working, of course, but he would be just as kind—and he was a good deal more entertaining. She smiled and someone said: 'Oh, lord, we'll have to give you a wedding present.'

Serena put down her cup. 'No, oh no, you mustn't—I don't know when—there's nothing settled.'

'Time to save up,' said someone else. 'Give us plenty of warning, Serena.'

They all laughed and presently dispersed to their various duties, and Serena, caught up in the usual afternoon rush, had no time to think about herself.

She got off duty late too, so that the half-formed idea that she would write home and tell her parents came to nothing. Time enough, she argued as she got ready for bed, when she went home the following weekend.

She had two letters from Laurens within the next few days—gay, extravagantly worded trifles which she read a dozen times and put under her pillow, as though, in her sleep, she could still read them. His mother, he wrote, would be delighted to have her as a guest for as long as she liked to stay; he would give her details of the exact date later on, and he was hers for ever, Laurens.

She didn't say anything to her mother until the morning after her arrival at the rectory—somehow it had been impossible during the evening before, with all the odds and ends of family news to exchange and a great deal of time taken up by Susan, who wanted to describe her latest boy-friend. They were in the kitchen, she and her mother, getting the midday meal, when she seized the opportunity to say: 'Mother, you remember the Dutch doctor?'

Her mother didn't look up from her pastry-making. 'Yes, indeed I do. Such a charming young man and so large and quiet. . .'

'Oh, not him,' said Serena impatiently, 'I mean the other one, the patient—the one who had the accident.'

Mrs Potts turned her pastry on to the wooden table top and looked at her daughter. 'Yes, dear?'

'Well, he's gone home,' Serena was finding it very difficult and she didn't know why, 'and he's coming back again in three weeks' time—to pick up his car, you know. He wants me to—to go to

Holland and stay with his mother. I think he wants to marry me.'

Her mother picked up the rolling pin and proceeded to roll her pastry. 'Yes, dear—how very quick young people are to make up their minds these days. And are you going to?'

'I don't know,' and then with a sudden rush of honesty, 'Yes, I do know, Mother. I am going to.' She went on rapidly, slightly on the defensive although her mother had said nothing to make her so: 'I'm sure he'll come down and see you and Father when he comes over; you'll like him—he's fun, and—and he's charming, and. . .'

'You love him, darling?'

'Oh, Mother, I'm sure I do—everything seems different.'

Mrs Potts transferred the rolled out pastry from the table to the pie dish and started a complicated patternwork around its edge.

'Your father and I will be delighted to meet—what's his name—Laurens, when he comes, and I'm happy that you're so happy, Serena, just as your father will be. When do you plan to marry?'

'Well, we aren't engaged; I expect he wanted me to go to his home first and meet his mother, but he's asked me to resign from Queen's. . .'

'You've not done that?' Her mother's voice was a thought sharp.

Serena was too deep in her own excited thoughts to have noticed. 'Oh, yes,' she answered airily, 'I have. I—I don't think Laurens wants to wait. There's no need; I don't know for certain, but I think his practice is a good one.'

'His cousin is a partner?'

'Yes, but I should think that Laurens is the one who does most of the work.'

'Why do you say that, Serena?'

'Well, his cousin. . .' she stopped, for actually she had no evidence that Gijs was lazy or not very clever at his work, rather to the contrary; only little joking remarks Laurens had made from time to time. And Gijs had been very good with the battered baby. 'I daresay I'm wrong,' she finished. 'It's just that he seems so leisurely, if you see what I mean.'

'A good man to have with you in a tight corner, all the same,' pronounced her mother, 'but I daresay Laurens is just as sound a man.' She put the pie in the oven. 'Let's go and tell your father.'

If the Reverend Mr Potts was surprised at his eldest child's news, he gave no sign; he said all that was expected of him, forbore from asking tedious questions, and added his assurance to his wife's that he would be delighted to welcome Laurens at the earliest opportunity. They had finished their conversation and had wandered out into the garden when he asked gently:

'What do you know of his family, my dear?'

'Not much,' replied Serena. 'They live in this town—Zierikzee—it's small and old. I don't know exactly where Laurens lives—whether the surgery is one he shares with his cousin in the town and he lives somewhere else; I never thought to ask.'

'And you've received an invitation from his mother?'

'No, not a written one, but surely she will write—I can't very well go without, can I?'

'There's no reason why you shouldn't, since it's your future husband who wishes you to visit his home. I daresay I'm a little old-fashioned, but. . .'

Serena squeezed his arm. 'No, you're not, darling, and I wouldn't dream of going unless I get a letter.'

She went back to hospital after her weekend with a great deal to think about, for naturally, both her mother and sisters were already discussing the wedding; was it to quiet, or, as her mother suggested a little wistfully, a nice country wedding like Margery's with all their friends and family and Laurens's family as well, then Serena could wear all a bride's trappings. . . Serena secretly hoped for that too, she spent the journey back to London thinking about it—organza, she decided happily, made up very simply, and a net veil. The train journey had never passed so swiftly.

She wrote to Laurens that evening, telling him that she had been home and told her parents about her visit to him, but she said no more than that. And when he didn't write for several days she wondered if perhaps she had been too hasty—perhaps she should have waited and told them when he came over to fetch her, but then that would have been secretive and there was nothing to be secretive about. Her doubts were put at rest by the sight of a letter with a Dutch postmark upon it the following morning, although she was unable to read it at once; she had to wait until it was coffee time and she had a few minutes to herself. She had just taken the letter from its envelope when Mr Thompson walked in, to stay, drinking coffee, discussing a nasty lacerations of foot they had just dealt with. He then went on to discuss the weather, the appalling food in the hospital canteen, the breakdown of the middle-aged car he ran, and finally asked if she had heard any more from the Dutchman whose leg he had seen.

Serena answered cautiously that yes, she had; he

seemed to be going on very well, even with his plaster.

'Oh, well,' said Mr Thompson, 'it was only a Pott's, wasn't it? He'll be able to shed his plaster very soon now. Back to work, is he?'

'I don't know.'

'He's lucky to have that cousin of his to run the practice,' said Mr Thompson forthrightly, and stared at her hard, so that she felt compelled to say: 'Oh, all right, Tom, you're dying to ask me if the grape-vine's true, aren't you? Well, it is. I'm leaving—and I'm going to Holland, just for a visit.'

'Then why are you leaving?' he pounced. 'Surely. . .' he stopped, looking uncomfortable. 'It's not my business. We shall all miss you, Serena.' He got up. 'All the best, though, in case I don't get the chance to say it in private before you go.'

He was sweet, but she barely wasted a second on him. She should really go back to the Accident Room, but she had to read Laurens's letter first. It was, as usual, brief and amusing and said nothing at all—at least, nothing of the things she wanted to know. Serena refolded it slowly and went back to her work and was fortunate enough to be so busy that she had no time to give her own affairs so much as a thought. Only that evening, when she went off duty, she went to her room instead of joining the others in the sitting-room and sat down on her bed to think. That she was very much in love with Laurens she had no doubt, and that he was in love with her she was almost as certain, but perhaps he didn't want to get married, at least for some time, despite what he had said. Perhaps she had been too transparent, too eager—men didn't like to be chased. She decided, upon reflection, that she hadn't been either and felt a little better. Perhaps he was a man to hide his deeper feelings under a lighthearted manner. . . She got off the bed and went to take a bath, to be stopped on the way by Joan tearing along at a great rate. 'There you are!' she exclaimed, a bit out of breath. 'There's someone on the phone for you—Holland, they said—here, give me those— it's the box at the bottom of the stairs.'

It was Laurens; all Serena's doubts and worries melted at the sound of his voice; they disappeared entirely when he told her that his mother had sent her an invitation to stay, 'And I'll be over on the first of May, so be ready for me, my gipsy girl,' he finished.

'Yes,' said Serena breathlessly, and added: 'But must we go straight away? I wondered if you would like to go down to my home and meet my mother and father.'

She hardly noticed his pause. 'Not this time, darling girl—we could visit them later on. They don't mind you coming?'

She said no, wondering as she said it what exactly her parents' feelings had been, trying to rid herself of the idea that they weren't quite. . .but then they hadn't met Laurens. When they did they would have no reservations at all. She told him that she would do exactly as he wished and was rewarded by the warmth of his voice. 'I'll be over some time in the evening. I shall fly, of course, pick up the car and fetch you the following morning. We shall be back here by tea time.'

'You're sure your mother wants. . .' began Serena, and was instantly hushed into security by his. 'Of course she does—you'll have her letter in the morning. Now I must go, darling girl, I've friends waiting. 'Bye.'

The days passed, some fast, some slow, according to how busy she was at her work. Laurens didn't telephone again, but he wrote, less often now, but as he explained to her, he was back at work and a busy man. His mother had written too, a stiff, short letter containing a formal invitation and nothing more. Serena thought that probably she found it difficult to express herself in another language. She answered it with a nice little letter of her own and telephoned her mother to tell her about it. Mrs Potts' voice very youthful-sounding over the wire, exclaimed: 'Oh, good—then you'll be coming home before you go, won't you, dear?—and Laurens.'

Serena explained about Laurens. 'But I'll be coming myself next weekend,' she declared, 'and he says we'll come down later.'

She had felt relief when her mother merely remarked cheerfully: 'That will be nice, darling,' and not mentioned it again.

There were still several days to go before she went home when she decided to do the last of her shopping one morning; she wasn't on until one o'clock and there were one or two things she needed to buy and it was a lovely morning to be out. She took a bus to Oxford Street and spent an hour there spending rather more money than she had intended and enjoying herself hugely, so that by the time she called a halt she discovered that it was a good deal later than she had thought. The Underground was the answer, for she was passing Marble Arch subway. Within a few minutes she was on a Central Line train—it would take her to Aldgate and from there it was only a few minutes' walk to Queen's.

They were between the Bank and Aldgate when the lights went out. The train came to a sudden halt and its occupants were thrown untidily against each other while a few unfortunates, standing near the doors waiting to get out, fell against less yielding objects. Serena, who had been sitting between a fat woman and a smartly dressed matron who had been shopping like herself, found herself on the floor with a good deal of the fat woman on top of her and the smart matron, rather surprisingly, indulging in instant hysterics.

It was amazing how hopeless it was to do anything in total darkness; she was still clutching her parcels and her bag, hanging from its shoulder strap. The noise, if anything, was worse now and the dark profound. Serena swallowed rising panic and wondered if anyone felt as terrified as she did. If only she had a lighter, but she didn't smoke—perhaps the fat woman could help. She bellowed her request in that lady's ear and rather surprisingly had success. There were matches in her coat pocket—'With me fags,' explained a breathy voice in her ear. 'Put yer 'and in, ducks, and get 'em out.'

Serena did so, thankful that her companion showed no signs of panic. The pocket held an assortment of nameless objects, but the matches were there all right. Serena struck one and held it aloft. Its tiny glimmer served to light only a small part of the chaos around her, but at least it encouraged other people to do the same; within seconds there were matches being struck, and lighters, rather more lasting, were held aloft, their combined feeble rays merely serving to make the chaotic conditions around her rather worse. It was at that precise moment that she became aware of three things—

that there were moans coming from the far end of
the coach, that there was a faint smell of burning,
and that she had a splitting headache. They all
needed looking into, but first things first. She turned
her head, wincing, and spoke into the dark on
her left.

'There's someone hurt,' she shouted at the fat
woman. 'I think I'd better go and see if I can help—
I'm a nurse.' She pushed her parcels and handbag
into the capacious lap beside her. 'Will you mind
these, please?'

'OK, ducks. Which 'ospital?'

'Queen's. Look, stay where you are whatever happens, you'll be safe.' She turned her head the other
way. 'And you be quiet,' she commanded fiercely
to the sobbing and shrieking matron. 'Can't you see
you're making it worse than it is already?'

She got up and started down the coach, a difficult
business because although no one had anywhere to
go, they seemed unable to keep still. She was perhaps
half way there when someone ahead of her shouted
urgently:

'Hi—someone, there's a man hurt!' and hard on
that cry came another one—a woman's voice this
time, raised in a thin scream. 'Fire—I smell fire!'

'Oh, shut up,' said Serena to the mass of people
around her, her own panic quite drowned in the
urgency to reach whoever it was who was moaning.
It was a pity that the smell of burning had now
become unmistakable. Her exquisite nose twitched
and a shiver of fear ran down her spine, made worse
by the concerted rush by almost everyone in the
coach to go somewhere. That there was nowhere to
go didn't for the moment matter, the general idea
was to get out; it would of course have been much

easier if the darkness hadn't made it impossible for anyone to find the doors, which wouldn't open anyway. Serena, pushing slowly forward, heard glass break and hoped that no one had been caught in the splinters or been foolish enough to get out on to the line, although surely by now someone, somehow, would have got a message to the station ahead of them and the current would be cut off—the driver must have reached Aldgate and given the alarm.

She made a final effort and found that the moans were coming from the floor directly in front of her feet, but it took a good deal of pushing and shoving to get down to that level because no one wanted to make room for her and the unfortunate on the floor had either been forgotten or considered past help. At last a man, holding his lighter above his head, realized what she was trying to do and cleared a tiny space for her.

The man on the floor was in a bad way, and she saw no chance of moving him. One leg was twisted under him and he had a nasty gash on his face, probably caused by someone's heel. She looked up at the man with the lighter and called urgently: 'We've got to move him. . .' but the man shook his head, although by now one or two people were trying to help—but it needed more than one or two people. She crouched over him, telling him that he would be all right and that help was on its way, although he couldn't hear a word of what she was saying. At that moment there was a vivid flash, a loud bang, and the sound of fire crackling, and the homely sound wasn't homely at all, but there, in the dark, quite terrifying.

Until that moment, although there had been a good deal of shouting and pushing and confusion, no one, with the exception of the smart matron, had given way to panic, but now Serena from her crouching position on the floor could sense the panic rising around her; she felt panicky herself. If only it wasn't so dark. . . As though in answer a great beam of light was shone through the broken windows of the coach and a cheerful voice called:

'We're opening the doors at this end. Come out slowly, there's plenty of time and help to get you to the station.'

It was a pity that someone, over-anxious to reach safety, began to push from the rear of the coach; the urge to escape suddenly became frantic and several people went down before it. It took longer to clear everyone out than it need have done and even then there were several people lying prone. Serena lifted her head cautiously and peered at the man she had been shielding. He seemed no worse, but he certainly couldn't have been any better. She was relieved to hear a voice—a nice cheerful voice, from the doors.

'Looks as though we'd better get the medicos down 'ere,' it said. 'Pass the word along, Bill.' The owner of the voice came inside the coach and Serena called: 'I don't know about the others, but this man's got a broken leg. . .'

She was interrupted by voices and a number of figures carrying powerful torches. There were women's voices too, she recognized Betsy's rather high penetrating tones and called thankfully:

'Betsy—there's a man here!'

It was nice to see Betsy, looking competent and beautifully normal. She dropped on her knees beside Serena, gave her a quick look and called over her shoulder: 'Can I have a doctor here, please?' then turned her attention to the man.

Serena became aware that someone else had
joined them. Doctor Gijs van Amstel. Betsy's torch-
light picked out his large feet as he came to a stop
beside them, and although his face was in gloom,
Serena had no doubt that he looked as placid as he
usually did. There was nothing placid about his
actions though; she felt herself scooped up and
carried away even while she was protesting that
she was fine and what about the man with the
broken leg?

He took no notice of her at all, but as he passed
the group of people bent over the victims scattered
around the coach he said: 'Bill, there's a man at the
other end needs help, fast. Betsy's there. I'll take
Serena straight back.'

Serena heard Bill exclaim: 'Serena, good lord!'
and twisted a little in the doctor's powerful arms. 'I
won't go,' she mumbled, and then contradicted herself by saying: 'I've got such an appalling headache.'

'I'm not surprised,' remarked Doctor van Amstel,
and started off down the track towards the station
whose platform had been turned into a kind of first
aid post; people were being treated, bandaged
roughly and dispatched to Queen's, but Serena
couldn't see much of what was going on, and anyway the ache over her eye was fast becoming the
only thing that mattered. She heard the doctor say
something briefly as he tramped down the platform
and through the barrier, up the stairs into the street
where he shouted at a waiting ambulance, bundled
her inside, shut the door on her and disappeared.

There were several other people in the ambulance,
but no one spoke, and the journey was a short one.
She was helped into the Accident Room, feeling all
of a sudden very shaky, and was received with cries

of surprised horror by her part-time staff nurse, who exclaimed:

'Sister, your head! You ought to be lying down—for heaven's sake!'

'I've only got a headache,' Serena explained. 'If I could sit down for a little while—Do go and see to the others, you must be up to your eyes.'

'We are—but there's plenty of staff.' Serena found herself being helped to one of the curtained-off bays, stretched out on its examination table while one of the student nurses arranged a paper towel beneath her head. 'Why,' she inquired fretfully, 'are you making all this fuss?'

'Just a small cut,' said Staff soothingly. 'Nothing much I'll get it cleaned up and someone will come and put a stitch in it.'

Serena put up her hand and felt a sticky tangle of hair, then remembered how often she had besought patients not to touch their injuries. She said: 'Sorry—I shouldn't have done that,' and was surprised to find that her hand was not only filthy dirty but covered in blood as well.

'All mine?' she wanted to know, and heard Staff laugh. 'I'm afraid so, it looks awful, but it's not too bad—here's Doctor van Amstel.'

'Why?' asked Serena, her eyes closed against the headache but dying of curiosity.

'I was here with Tom.' He was standing beside her while her head was being cleaned up. 'It seemed sensible to go along with him as a couple of men in the emergency team were in theatre. You'll need a stitch or two—you must have had a crack on the head. . .'

'My bag,' said Serena urgently, suddenly remembering and taking no notice of him at all. 'The fat woman had it—and my parcels. . .'

'We'll see about them presently. Now keep still while I give you a local.'

He was gentle and unhesitating, but it seemed a long time. 'How many stitches?' she wanted to know, and made to sit up with a jerk when he told her quietly: 'Eight—you had a nasty cut from your eyebrow to your malar bone.'

Serena muttered 'Oh,' then was very sick, and Doctor van Amstel dealt with that with the same gentle deliberation that he had displayed while he had been stitching her. 'You'll feel better now,' he observed calmly. 'Staff's gone to get you an anti-tetanus injection and you'd better have a shot of penicillin—Tom will write it up, I daresay. I don't think I should.'

Staff came back then, and Miss Stokes with her, and Serena muttered crossly: 'I'm on duty at one o'clock,' and heard him say:

'It's not for me to suggest, but I'm sure her MO will want her in bed for a couple of days and then a few days' rest before she comes back to duty. I believe Mr Thompson is arranging for an X-ray.'

'I don't want an X-ray,' Serena interrupted abruptly. 'I'm perfectly OK I didn't lose conscious-ness.' It was Miss Stokes who answered her.

'The doctor's gone, Sister Potts, but I'm sure he's right—I'll get Doctor Forsythe down as soon as I can and someone will help you to bed just as soon as you've been X-rayed.'

The next hour was a little blurred; X-ray, and being taken over to the Home and helped to bed and swallowing tablets, then told to go to sleep. . . She did, most thankfully, and wakened to find Mr Forsythe in the room. When he saw that she was awake he said briskly: 'Ah, good. What it is to be young and tough! No fracture, and that cut will heal in a few days; it's been stitched very nicely by our colleague from Holland. Two days in bed, young lady, and then a few days at home—stitches out after the fifth day and you'll be back at work again, none the worse.'

She listened to this heartening speech while something worrying niggled at the back of her mind. Mr Forsythe had been gone for some few minutes when she discovered what it was; if she had sick leave now, she wouldn't be able to leave at the end of the month. Her trip to Holland would have to be postponed, for she would have to make up the days she would be off sick before she could leave. She would have to let Laurens know as soon as possible. She lay awake worrying herself into another headache again, so that when Home Sister came presently to see how she was, she had to swallow some more tablets.

She felt better in the morning, partly because she was sure that Gijs van Amstel would come and see her or at least send a message. But he didn't come, and when Betsy poked her head round the door half way through the morning and Serena asked her if she would give him a message it was to be told that he had gone back to Holland the night before.

Serena was still wondering about Laurens. Of course Gijs would tell him as soon as he got back to Holland, she hadn't thought of that. She smiled, feeling relieved and said quite cheerfully: 'Oh. Now I must have a look. . .'

'Oh, time enough,' Betsy spoke rather too quickly. 'You're to stay in bed, remember?'

But when she had gone, Serena got out of bed

and pottered over to the mirror, wondering why she hadn't done so sooner; perhaps she hadn't felt sufficiently interested. Her reflection was hardly a reassuring one—the cut was hideous although it had been most carefully stitched, but it would leave a scar. It didn't worry her too much, but she couldn' help but wonder if Laurens would feel the same way, for she imagined that to him beauty had to be perfect, and her face was no longer perfect.

It was two days later and she had packed her bag ready to go home for a few days when the Home maid came in with a message to ask her to go downstairs as there was a gentleman to see her. Serena, to whom the last two days had been like two years because she had had no news from Laurens, went a delicious pink and squashing a desire to tie a scarf over her stitches, tore downstairs. It would be Laurens; she flung the door of the visitors' room open, her face radiant and stopped short. 'Oh, it's you,' she said, and went even pinker because she had been rude. 'I'm sorry,' she stammered, 'I thought it was. . .'

Gijs van Amstel smiled faintly. 'He couldn't manage it,' he told her cheerfully, 'so he asked if I'd slip over and see how things were. He's—er—very sorry. He asked me to give you these. . .' He waved towards an extravagant cellophane-wrapped sheaf of flowers. 'He also asked me to drive you home.'

She eyed the flowers with pleasure and answered somewhat absent-mindedly: 'Oh, that's quite unnecessary, I'm quite all right, except for this.' She put a hand up to her cheek and then dropped it again hurriedly in case he might think that she was fishing for sympathy. She need not have worried, for he said merely: 'I'm sure you are, but Laurens particularly asked me.'

'Yes, did he?' She smiled warmly, not at him, but at the idea of Laurens cherishing her. 'Then I'd better do as he asks, hadn't I?' She looked at him directly. 'Why are you over here so often?'

He answered without hesitation. 'Laurens isn't really fit to travel yet and he can't drive for another week or so. There's a certain amount of coming and going necessary to get his accident settled and the new car. . .' he was a little vague about the car, but she hadn't noticed, she was thinking that with so much time on his hands he must be a very unimportant member of the partnership.

'Shall we go?' His quiet inquiry disturbed her train of thought and she nodded at once. 'I'll get my things and come out to the car, shall I?'

She didn't wait for his reply but slipped back to her room, still thinking about Laurens.

She found Gijs waiting for her just outside the door. He took her bag saying, 'I left the car over here,' nodded vaguely to his left and started off with her following him through the parked cars, and when he stopped beside a dark blue Bentley, she said in a friendly voice because she had been rather cavalier in her treatment of him: 'What a gorgeous car! Don't you wish you were driving it?' She looked round her. 'I can't see the Mini. . .'

He put down her bag and produced some keys from a pocket; he sounded diffident when he spoke. 'Well, no—it's not here, we're going in this car.'

She goggled at him, then, anxious not to hurt his feelings because he really was the kindest of men, she said: 'Oh, has the Mini come to grief? Did you borrow this one? She's super, don't you find a lot of difference in driving it?'

He put her bag in the boot and closed it. 'No, not really—I've driven a Bentley before.' He opened the door for her and she got in. He must have some good friends if they lent him a Bentley, or perhaps Laurens had told him to hire it. She didn't like to ask and it was obvious that he wasn't going to tell her any more. She settled down in the comfortable seat as he got in beside her. Even in a car of that size, there seemed to be a great deal of him.

The car slid smoothly through the hospital fore-court and out into the busy street and Gijs asked: 'How many days have you?'

'Five—far too many, for I have to make them up, you know. That means I can't get away until a week later than we had planned.'

'Very disappointing,' he spoke casually, 'and I'm sure Laurens is just as disappointed. He'll be over to fetch you, though. I was to tell you that and to explain why he hadn't written—the practice is a busy one—babies and so forth,' he added.

Serena smiled to herself, conjuring up a picture of Laurens hard at work despite his leg. 'I'm sure it is,' she agreed. 'Does he have any helpers—other than you,' she added hastily.

'Oh, yes. A secretary and a surgery nurse and a couple of receptionists.'

She sat silent, watching her companion pilot the car through the city traffic. It must be a big practice; she would have liked to have asked about it, but perhaps it would be better to wait until she was there and could see it for herself. Her musings were checked by her companion remarking: 'I thought we might go over Salisbury and through Blandford.

There's a good place there where we might have lunch—the Crown, I daresay you know it.'

She hastened to accept and discovered that she was enjoying herself; he hadn't once commented upon the hideous little scar with its shiny black stitches standing up like miniature barbed wire; indeed, he hadn't mentioned the accident, nor inquired after her health; but he was taking the trouble to drive her home. She felt, for the first time in several days, relaxed, and at the same time she found herself surprised that he was such good company. Why, she wondered, hadn't she noticed that when he had driven her up to London?

They ate their lunch in a most friendly atmosphere, talking trivialities which she suspected he was deliberately keeping to. They ate ham off the bone accompanied by a delicious salad and new potatoes, and followed it with apple pie and cream and drank sparingly of a dry white wine which Serena, ignorant of such things, nevertheless found exactly right. She said so, and Gijs twinkled nicely at her and thanked her for her approval. Her answering smile was a little crooked by reason of the scar which still hurt, and it was then that she noticed for the first time that his eyes weren't blue like Laurens's, but grey.

She asked suddenly: 'You're older than Laurens, aren't you?' and watched his lips twitch as he answered blandly: 'Quite a good deal older. I'm thirty-six. And you,' he added deliberately, 'are twenty-four.'

For some reason this made her feel uncomfortable; it was as though he implied that she was in quite another age group than his own and that she had been impertinent to ask him in the first place. Well, she had been a little rude, she told herself honestly, and he had every right to be snooty about it.

They arrived at the Rectory in time for tea and it wasn't until they were seated round the table enjoying the substantial meal her mother considered desirable that Serena remarked suddenly: 'You know, I really am awful—I never telephoned you, did I? Supposing someone had gone all the way to Dorchester to meet the train. I can't think how I forgot.'

It was her mother who answered. 'Never mind, darling, I'm sure you still feel rotten. Doctor van Amstel rang your father this morning, so we knew you were coming by car.' She caught the sparkle in her daughter's fine eyes and added swiftly: 'Very thoughtful of you, Doctor,' and because her daughter's eyes were still smouldering: 'Do have some more of this cake, Susan made it. Her young man— no, I have to say boy-friend, don't I?—likes a domesticated girl, so she does most of the cooking at the moment because Eric comes to supper most evenings.'

'Eric?' queried Serena, instantly diverted. 'I thought his name was Bert.'

Susan, from across the table, sitting beside their visitor, snorted and tossed her hair over her shoulder. 'Serena, he was ages ago—besides, he didn't like dogs.'

Serena took another slice of cake and said understandingly: 'Oh, well, in that case he wouldn't do at all.' The Rectory housed two dogs and several cats as well as an odd rabbit or two, a hedgehog and a barn owl who came and went when he liked.

'You have a dog of your own, Doctor van Amstel?' the rector inquired.

The big man smiled at his host. 'A dog—yes, a

dachshund called, with a great lack of imagination, I'm afraid, German. There is a cat too, called Hemel, because that is what I said when I first saw him.'

'What does *hemel* mean?' demanded Susan, making play with her eyelashes.

'Heavens—he is actually a very earthy beast, though.' They all laughed, and Serena, looking round the table, sensed that they all liked the doctor, which was wonderful because it meant that they would like Laurens even better; was he not younger? She was going to add 'and more amusing', but all at once she wasn't quite sure about that.

He went soon after tea and they stood, clustered round the porch, watching him get into the car, but before he did so he turned back and came to a halt before Serena. 'Dear me, I almost forgot—I shall be coming for you in five days' time. I might just as well, I have to come to England once more. The next time it will be Laurens.'

She had no time to reply, only wave with the others as the big car skimmed up the hill towards the main road. She wondered why he had reminded her that it would be Laurens who would be fetching her. Did he really suppose that she would forget?

The five days went quickly; there was always so much to do at home, she found, and time enough to do it in. She was nicely tanned by the time the last day came and the scar, its stitches ready to come out, didn't seem to matter at all, perhaps because no one ever mentioned it. She helped her mother about the house, and cooked a little and found the time to do some knitting and reading and take the dogs for long walks. When the last morning came she felt regret, but it was mixed with excitement because very soon she would be seeing Laurens again.

This time Gijs van Amstel wasn't early but exactly on time, moreover he had breakfasted on the way, so there was nothing for it but to get into the Bentley without delay, smiling with determined cheerfulness until the rectory and the little group at its front door were no longer to be seen.

They were almost in Dorchester when the doctor said: 'You look very well—presumably the stitches come out the moment you get back. Will you think it unpardonable of me if we don't stop for lunch? I have several things to do and I'm going back today.' He turned to smile at her. 'Coffee, though—I should think we might reach the Hog's Back round about eleven.'

Serena said how nice and felt disappointed; she had expected, or at least hoped, that he would take her out to lunch again. She had enjoyed the homeward trip, but then there had been no hurry; apparently today there was. She said, faintly waspish: 'You really shouldn't have come—it's such a waste of time for you and I could perfectly well have gone by train.'

'Ah, yes, I know that, but remember Laurens asked me.' A remark which made Serena fume silently, for it sounded as though her companion had made the journey merely to do a service for his cousin and not because he enjoyed her company. But why, she asked herself reasonably, should he enjoy her company? Had he not once asked her why she disliked him and had she ever given him any real answer? She said woodenly: 'It's very kind of you to put yourself out,' and was enraged afresh by his idle: 'Yes, isn't it, but I'm a kind man when it suits me.'

It was quite a relief when he drew up in front of

the hospital, helped her out, fetched her bag from
the boot and went to the entrance with her, where
he bade her a rather abrupt goodbye with the kind
of lazy courtesy she had come to expect from him.
She went over to her room feeling strangely let
down, and even the sight of her healed face when
the stitches had been taken out did little to restore
her cheerfulness. She unpacked and went down to
a late dinner, assuring herself that she didn't wish
to see too much of Gijs van Amstel while she was
in Holland, for despite his casual air, he disturbed
her strangely.

CHAPTER FOUR

SERENA had expected the time to drag; that the days would seem endless before she would leave Queen's and go to Holland, but it was nothing of the sort; the Accident Room had never been so busy, and Laurens, who had written so seldom at first, was now writing or telephoning every day. She packed, gave a farewell party to her friends and staff, paid a duty visit to the Matron's office and found herself, at last, dressed and ready and waiting for Laurens. He was to fetch her during the early afternoon, for they were to travel on the evening ferry. It would get them to Zeebrugge by half past ten or so and there was only the matter of an hour or so's drive after that.

The weather was still very warm and sunny and Serena was wearing a sleeveless blue dress with a little jacket in case it got chilly in the evening. Her scar still showed pinkly against the tan of her face, but it had healed well, thanks to Gijs' neat stitchery, with no pucker to mar its line—in a month or so it would be, if not invisible, almost so. It didn't worry her any more—nothing worried her, life was perfect and the future a delightful dream yet to be lived. She took a last look round her room with a small pang of regret, because she had been happy there, and went down to the hospital entrance, exactly at the time Laurens had asked her to be there. He was waiting; her heart gave a thud of happiness at the sight of him and quickened its beat as he got out of the car—the new Jag—and came towards her. There were plenty of people about; nurses going to and fro, consultants arriving, housemen hanging around waiting for their chiefs, but none of them deterred Laurens from kissing her in a most satisfying, if brief, manner, only the moment marred just a little for her when he held her back from him to study her face intently.

'Not bad,' he decided. 'A pity it had to mar your lovely face, but Gijs has done a neat job, I must say,' and then as though he sensed her feelings, hurried on: 'and how are you after all this time, my beautiful gipsy? More beautiful than ever, I can see that, despite the scar—let's hope it fades quickly, and thank heaven it wasn't right on your cheek, at least it doesn't show too badly. . .'

Serena, still breathless from the kiss, felt a small prick of dismay; it seemed to her that the scar didn't matter at all. Surely if you loved someone, you loved them, not their looks? She dismissed the worrying thought and gave him a dazzling smile. 'It will have faded in another week or two,' she assured him. 'I've heaps of luggage.'

While he was stowing it she asked: 'How's your leg?'

'Almost a hundred per cent. Gijs wasn't too keen on me driving back, but it hardly bothers me at all. Besides, it's my business what I do.'

He looked so sulky that she hastened to say something. 'Are you working too hard?'

'I'm not working at all, my beauty—I shall start this week.'

She got in beside him, remembering with an unwelcome clarity that Gijs had told her that Laurens couldn't come to see her because he was working so hard. She pushed that thought away too, to join the one about the scar; probably she was being over-sensitive and she could easily have mistaken what Gijs had told her.

It was the clear dark of a summer night when they landed in Belgium, and there was still quite a lot of traffic about, although this didn't deter Laurens from tearing along the uneven cobbled roads as though he were on a race track, and when they had crossed the border into Holland, and the roads were smooth and fast except in the towns where they were brick, he went even faster. 'We'll be in by midnight,' he assured her confidently, and they were, because they had caught the ferry at Breskens by the skin of their teeth, saving themselves half an hour's wait.

Serena peered around her, but there wasn't a great deal to see. In the semi-dark the flat land and sky merged into each other so that there was no horizon; it seemed no time at all when Laurens said in a pleased voice:

'Here we are,' and shot down a left-hand turn off the main road. 'I live on the outside of the town,' Laurens told her. 'The house isn't so very old, late eighteenth century—some of the houses in the town go back a couple of hundred years more than that.'

He swung the car into a narrow road and then turned again down a short lane, wide enough to take a car and no more. There were gates at its end standing open; he shot through them rather too fast and stopped outside the porched doorway of a solid square house. 'Here we are,' he remarked, and looked at his watch, 'and in good time too.'

He got out and opened the door and they went through it together. 'In you go, my beauty,' he told her. 'I'll get the bags later. Mother will be in bed but Sieska will be about somewhere.'

He pushed her gently into the hall and closed the door. The hall was dimly lit, but she could see that it was square and lofty, with a staircase ascending up one side of it. There was a light coming from the half open door close to her and Laurens directed: 'In here, Serena, I'll go and see what Sieska's got for us.'

She went through the door ahead of him, feeling strangely let down at their lack of welcome, although her common sense told her that their arrival was so late that her hostess could be forgiven for going to bed. All the same. . .

It was obviously a sitting-room, large and lofty-ceilinged and furnished a little heavily and with solid comfort. After the shabby Rectory, Serena found it a little awe-inspiring and far less welcoming. There were a pair of table lamps shining a rather tepid greeting and Laurens, following her in, said: 'Gloomy, eh? I'm going to find some food and coffee.'

He came back presently with a tray of coffee and sandwiches which they consumed without much talk and when he said: 'Well, my gipsy, what about bed?' she was only too ready to comply; she would have a good sleep and in the morning everything would be all right. He fetched her luggage and they went quietly upstairs to a square landing, its walls pierced at regular intervals by doors, one of which Laurens opened and ushered her inside. The room was long, narrow, and again, high-ceilinged. It had a green carpet, furniture of satinwood which was almost as heavy as that in the sitting-room, and it smelled very clean, of polish and lavender and methylated spirit, it also smelled as though no one had slept in it for a very long time.

'Don't know why Mother gave you this room,' Laurens commented. 'No one sleeps here much, but I don't suppose that will make any difference to you.' He put down her cases and turned to her, smiling. At least, Serena consoled herself a few minutes later, whatever the shortcomings of her welcome, there had been nothing wrong with his goodnight kiss.

She wakened to broad daylight and a gentle tapping on the door and a cheerful-faced girl came in with tea, smiled and nodded and went away again. Serena looked at her watch; it was eight o'clock. She drank her tea, dragged on her dressing gown and crossed the landing to the bathroom Laurens had pointed out to her the night before. She bathed without haste, dressed in the pale green dress she had worn in London and went downstairs, feeling uncertain. She was standing in the hall when Laurens came in from the garden, kissed her and took her arm. 'Mother never comes down to breakfast,' he told her. 'We'll have it now, shall we?'

He led her to a small room where a round table was spread ready for them, sat her down at it, poured coffee for them both and took a chair opposite her. Serena sipped the coffee, took a roll from the basket he offered and asked: 'Do you have a morning surgery?'

He shook his head. 'Gijs is doing almost all the work at the moment. I go in for the evening surgeries—I sit most of the time.'

'Your leg bothers you? Isn't it a bit soon to. . .'

'Lord, no—it aches a bit, but I've done this before, you know—an arm once too.' He shrugged.

'I've a stick to help me along and I'm having physio.'

'But driving all that way?'

'Don't get so worried, little gipsy Potts.' He sounded a little impatient; she helped herself experimentally to a slice of cheese—the Dutch ate cheese for breakfast, so if she was to become an adopted member of the van Amstel family, she had better cultivate a taste for it. 'Your mother?' she inquired tentatively.

'Oh, she'll be down presently,' he answered carelessly. 'Have you almost finished? I've a great deal of post to attend to, I think I'll go and get on with it while you finish, then we can have a look round.'

He strolled off, whistling, and she, left alone, lost her appetite for cheese. She was ladling sugar into her cup when the door did open and Laurens's mother came in. At least, it had to be his mother, because she was exactly like the image Serena had built up in her mind; tall and a little stout, with well dressed greying hair and his good looks; moreover she had a regal manner which left Serena in no doubt as to who was mistress of the household. The lady advanced to the table and Serena stood up.

'Miss Potts?' Somehow the crisp voice made her name sound ridiculous. 'You must forgive me for not staying up to welcome you, but it was a little late.' She smiled without warmth. 'Laurens has told me so much about you—I do hope that you will enjoy your little holiday with us.' She extended a hand and Serena shook it, hearing her own voice making suitable replies while her mind wrestled with the puzzle her hostess's words had given her. If she was here for a little holiday where was she supposed to go afterwards, and how long did a little holiday last? She would have to talk to Laurens urgently. He came in just then, kissed his mother, said easily: 'Oh, hullo, you two have met. Good,' and smiled at them both. 'I'm going to take Serena on a little tour of inspection, Mama.'

His mother nodded briefly. 'Of course, dear. Lunch will be at half past twelve. Remember that we have a few friends coming in this evening, won't you?' She turned to Serena. 'We live very quietly, although we do a little entertaining amongst our-selves. We must try and think up something to amuse you while you are with us, mustn't we?' She smiled at them both and went to the door. 'Don't be late for lunch,' she warned them, and closed the door quietly behind her.

Laurens flung an arm around Serena's shoulders. 'Fetch your bonnet and we'll go. A quick look at the town first, and further afield this afternoon.'

It hardly seemed the right moment to ask what his mother had meant. She fetched her handbag and joined him in the hall. She walked beside him round the house to what must have been the stables and was now the garage, then got into the Jag beside him and nodded happily when he said:

'We'll go round the outside of the town and through the Noordhavenpoort. You couldn't have seen much last night.'

The gate looked imposing by daylight. They drove slowly through its deep arch, with the funny little painted shuttered windows piercing the thickness of its walls, and into the Oude Haven, a wide cobbled street dissected by a canal. To the left of them was a white painted wooden bridge leading to the other side of the canal and yet another, smaller gate. The street was lined with houses, all different, some

large, some small; all old. Serena was still studying
them when Laurens drove slowly on to stop again
where the canal, filled in, had become a grassed
garden with a bandstand in its centre. Beyond it was
a cobbled market square, thick with parked cars.
'Look across the canal to the other side,' Laurens
advised her. 'There is Gijs's house.'

She followed his pointing hand—the houses were
packed tightly, all shapes and sizes. There was a
small one wedged between a larger gabled one and
a very much bigger one with a great door, whose
framework and that of the vast window above it was
surrounded by intricate plaster work. She turned her
attention to its small neighbour.

'The little one,' she stated.

'No—the one next to it.'

'Not the big one with the door?' She tried to keep
surprise out of her voice and failed, because the
house was so unlike her vague ideas of Gijs's home.
'Isn't it a little large?' she ventured.

'Vast, but it's been in his family for generations—
besides, he hates to be cramped. He suffered agonies
in that Mini.' Laurens laughed and she echoed him
uncertainly. 'Oh? isn't the Mini his?'

He laughed again. 'No—when you telephoned
about me, he got on the first flight and borrowed
the Mini—God knows who from. He's got friends in
the most unlikely places—some chap near London
Airport, I believe.'

'I see,' said Serena calmly, and fumed silently.
Gijs had deliberately misled her, and why? She
would find out when she saw him. 'Is the surgery
in his house?'

'No—in the centre of the town. Gijs sees his private patients at his own house, of course.' He turned

away, obviously a little bored with the whole subject, and she made haste to ask: 'What's that old building on the left?'

This time they drove down the other side of the canal and going past Gijs's house, Serena peered closely at its windows, hoping to get a glimpse of what might be inside, but although the windows were enormous they were discreetly veiled with pristine white net curtains, although the funny mumble of windows in the older wing of the house were open and uncurtained. She observed obliquely. 'It is a large house. Your cousin's wife must have quite a job. . .' because she knew he wasn't married, but Gijs might be engaged.

Laurens gave a shout of laughter. 'Gijs married, or even thinking of it? He's much too lazy, though I must say he's such a silent man when it comes to his own affairs.' He darted a quick look at her. 'In any case, I shouldn't tell on him.' Which remark caused her to redden painfully. Perhaps she had been too curious, but after all, if she was to marry Laurens surely it was natural for her to want to know about his family.

They were back in good time for lunch, which they had with Laurens's mother, who made polite and intelligent conversation on trivial matters in her excellent, rather stilted English. That she was very fond of her son was apparent and that he was able to twist her round his little finger was still more apparent. Serena ate without much appetite because she felt that something wasn't quite right and she didn't know what it was.

It wasn't until later that afternoon, as Laurens drove the Jag across the flat green island to Brouwershaven, that Serena found the opportunity to air her doubts. They had been talking about his return to work and she seized the chance to say: 'Talking of returning to work, Laurens, your mother—when we met this morning, you know—she spoke as though I had come just for a few days on a casual visit—as though I'm going back to Queen's. Does she know—about us, I mean?'

'Well, more or less. You see, it's been rather a surprise to her, darling. She needs to get used to the idea.'

'But she must have known when she wrote to me—doesn't she approve?'

'Oh, come now, I didn't say that.'

'No, I know you didn't, but she doesn't know we're going to get married, does she?' Serena turned to look at Laurens and saw his sulky expression, but when he pulled into the side of the road and stopped the car and turned to face her, she saw that he was smiling. 'Beautiful girl, aren't you being a little bit intense about it all? There's time enough to think about getting married—we hardly know each other.'

He flung an arm around her and she sat rigid under it. 'Are you telling me you've changed your mind?'

He laughed and bent to kiss her cheek. 'How ridiculous you are, and how lovely you look when you're cross—did you know? All I'm saying is, let's stay as we are for a week or two; when Mother gets to know you she'll be as crazy about you as I am.' He kissed her again and she, feeling foolish at her outburst, kissed him back; everything was perfectly all right after all. They had only known each other a very short time and there was no hurry. She smiled back at him and said contritely: 'I'm a fool, aren't I? Only I did want your mother to like me and I suppose I'm a bit nervous.'

She was rewarded by another kiss and for the rest of the afternoon he was cheerful and lighthearted and attentive to her every whim. They had tea in Haamstede, a pleasant little resort in the dunes on the other side of the island, and then went back to Zierikzee so that they would have time to change before the friends his mother had invited should arrive.

There was no one coming to dinner, Laurens had said, Serena went downstairs at seven o'clock, wearing a pink crêpe dress which fitted her slender person exactly and flared gently into a wide skirt. It had a chiffon frill at its deep V-neckline and because she hadn't any good jewellery she didn't wear any, only the keeper ring, but she had taken extra pains with her face and swept her well brushed hair into its usual simple topknot because she knew that it suited her that way. She hoped that Laurens would approve, and still more important, his mother.

The sitting-room door was a little open and she quickened her steps. The others must be already down—she opened the door wider and went in. Neither Laurens nor his mother were there, but Gijs was, standing, massive and quiet, before the empty hearth. He looked different, and it took her a few seconds to discover why—he was dressed differently. Now he wore a well tailored and elegant suit, perhaps a little conservative in cut but of a fine grey cloth; his tie was exquisite too, and he looked—she sought for a word and came up with wealthy, but that wouldn't do at all; that smacked of the ostentatious and Gijs could never be that. She broke the silence he hadn't attempted to break and said: 'Hullo, Gijs, I didn't know—that is, Laurens said that no one. . .'

He smiled faintly, looking down on her with a benign expression which annoyed her. 'Oh, but I don't count—I'm family, you see. I believe my aunt thought that four at dinner would be better than three.' He moved away from the hearth and came to stand in front of her. 'Enjoying yourself, I hope?'

He sounded no more than politely casual, but when she looked at him it was to encounter grey eyes which bored into hers with such intentness that she blinked under their stare. 'Very much, thank you, though I haven't seen much yet.'

He said without smiling: 'You have seen nothing yet.'

Which was a perfectly ordinary remark, but for some reason she found herself searching for its real meaning. She was still puzzling over it when Laurens came in with a casual greeting for his cousin and a warmer one for herself.

'Hullo. Mother not down yet? Have a drink, Serena. Sherry?'

She thanked him a little absentmindedly, accepted the glass he fetched for her and watched him pour gin and tonic for Gijs and then help himself. They were chatting idly when Laurens's mother came in. She was without doubt a handsome woman, the grey dress she was wearing, so simple and so expensive, put Serena's own dress completely in the shade and made her feel positively dowdy, an opinion shared by her hostess, if the brief appraising glance she cast at her as she settled herself in her chair was anything to go by. But her manner towards Serena was charming and gracious and remained so throughout dinner, even though she allowed no one to take the conversation out of her hands during the meal.

They had their coffee at table and then crossed

the hall to the double doors on its other side. The drawing-room, without a doubt, and a splendid one, with long wide windows hung richly with crimson brocade and a number of tables and chairs scattered about its carpeted floor. Serena found it a little stiff and formal, although the flowers in their vases on the wall tables were beautiful and most artistically arranged. There were a number of paintings on the walls too and she would have liked an opportunity to study them, but her hostess patted the sofa where she had seated herself and Serena felt impelled to go and sit beside her, a little envious of the men, who had gone to the further end of the room for some purpose of their own.

Her companion settled herself against the cushions. 'And now—Serena, is it not? Why do I have such difficulty in remembering your name, for I have had enough practice, I must admit, Laurens has so many girl-friends—' she laughed a little and Serena dutifully echoed her, because there was nothing else to do. 'Tell me about yourself. I know that you are a hospital Sister—a *Hoofd Zuster*, are you not?'

There seemed little point in telling her companion that she was no longer working in hospital. Serena replied: 'Yes,—I'm in charge of the Accident Room at Queen's—quite a big hospital in London, where Laurens went, as I'm sure you know. We're almost always busy, but it's work I like doing.'

'And your parents?'

'My father is a country rector. He and my mother live in a small village in Dorset.'

'Clergy,' mused her hostess *sotto voce*, and asked; 'Rector? Is that an important post in your church— a bishop, perhaps?'

'Heavens no, just an ordinary clergyman.'

'And your mother?'

Serena recognized that she was being vetted, and since she was going to be one of the family, she didn't resent it. 'She helps my father in the parish— she's always busy.' She smiled a little, thinking of that cheerful, practical lady with her never-ending enthusiasm for the day's tasks.

'The house is large, I expect?' The voice was gentle but persistent.

Serena fell neatly into the trap set for her. 'Oh, yes, Victorian at its worst and quite non-labour-saving. The housework's unending.'

'But living in the country, as she does, I'm sure your mother is able to obtain servants easily.'

'She does almost everything herself,' answered Serena, falling a little deeper into the trap. 'Mrs Palmer from the village comes in twice a week for an hour or so, but servants cost the earth in England.'

'Indeed? As they do in Holland.' Her companion's voice was pleasant, but Serena was uneasily aware that she had been got at. It was a relief when the men joined them and, a few minutes later, the first of the evening's guests.

There were quite a number; Laurens introduced her to the first half dozen or so and then turned to his duties as host, and when the group she was with drifted away one by one, she found herself standing alone, wishing that he would spare even a few minutes for her, for her hostess, beyond telling her to enjoy herself and remarking that Laurens would make sure that she met everyone, had drifted away to the opposite end of the room and was standing with her back to her. Apparently she had forgotten that she was there. Serena looked round her, searching for Laurens; he had forgotten her too. He was standing very close to a tall blonde girl, distinctly eye-catching and beautifully dressed. They were, she noticed, rage throbbing painfully in her breast, standing hand in hand. She tore her eyes away and met Gijs's steady look from the other side of the room; she turned her head away at once so that he shouldn't see the hurt surprise on her face.

He must have moved like lightning; she had taken two steps when his large hand came down firmly on her arm. She was conscious of relief as he said mildly: 'Keep me company in the garden, Serena— I'm not over-fond of these gatherings—such an effort to talk.' He smiled down at her lazily and there was no trace of pity, only faintly amused good nature. He had been propelling her towards the open window as he spoke and opened it wider for her to step through. Now she found herself outside in the warm evening air, the garden before her, his hand still on her arm, guiding her without haste around its formal beds and paths.

'Fantastic,' he murmured conversationally. 'This garden hasn't a blade of grass out of place—you should see mine.'

'Have you a garden?' Serena wasn't in the least interested, she was still seeing, far too clearly, Laurens standing hand in hand with the blonde.

'Yes, behind the house—you saw that, I expect?—it's very sheltered with a high stone wall. I enjoy an hour or so's gardening in it occasionally.'

The idea of her companion exerting himself to so much as pluck a weed momentarily diverted her thoughts. 'Oh? It doesn't seem quite your—your. . .' she didn't finish the sentence, but instead began a new, more urgent one.

'Who is she?' she asked.

He answered at once with a complete lack of surprise in his deep voice. It was as level and pleasant as it always was and Serena wondered crossly if he ever made the effort to be angry or unpleasant or surprised. Probably not.

'Adriana van Hoijden. They've known each other for years—brother and sister, you might say.'

'Does she live here—in Zierikzee?' Serena was aware that she was being foolish to let him see how upset she was, but she didn't care any more.

'In Haamstede—just outside the. . .'

'We went there this afternoon,' she interrupted him ruthlessly. 'What does she do?'

'Er—nothing that I know of. Money, you know, and an only child—poor girl. I'm sorry for only children, aren't you?'

She swallowed the next question because he so obviously wasn't going to answer it. 'Yes, I think I am.'

'Ah, at last I have found something about myself in which you can show some interest—I am an only child.'

She said woodenly, not caring in the least: 'I'm sorry. Did you find it very lonely?'

'When I was a little boy, yes. One learns as one older, however.' He turned her round and started to retrace their steps. 'And what do you think of Laurens's home?'

'It's—I haven't seen much of it yet. I've only been here a day.' It seemed longer.

'Ah, yes, so you have. You'll probably go on a conducted tour before very long. Is your stay a short one? I seem to remember asking you that before.'

'I don't know. . .'

'Surely not unlimited leave from the hospital?'

'I've left—you must know that, or can't you remember that either?' She sounded peevish and felt it.

'So you have, forgive me. I see that the scar is almost invisible. I'm glad—and may I add that you look delightful in that colour.'

He was only being kind, but at least he had admired her dress. Laurens hadn't even noticed it. She sighed and said thank you in a rather small voice, then heard him say: 'Well, we shall see, shall we not?'

They were approaching the house again. 'See what?' she wanted to know, but he didn't answer, which was infuriating of him, but led her inside again and stayed with her, collecting people around him with no apparent effort, until she was surrounded by a friendly little circle of people who all spoke English and seemed pleased to talk to her. When she looked round for Gijs presently, he had disappeared.

The evening was pleasanter after that; the circle widened and dwindled but never quite melted away, and presently Laurens joined it and remained until the guests began to leave. When the last of them had gone, Serena, standing with him at the still open window, asked: 'That pretty fair girl you were with, who was she? I didn't meet her.'

He took her arm. 'There weren't any pretty girls,' he said with satisfying fervour, 'only you,' which remark made it all the easier to say: 'Don't be ridiculous, Laurens. She was gorgeous. She had on a pale green dress with blue and green embroidery round the hem and down the front of the bodice. . .'

'You should have been a detective, darling. Now

I know who you mean. That was Adriana van Hoijden—I've known her for years, haven't seen her for ages—nice girl, if you like blondes.' He bent to kiss her. 'Personally, at this moment I have a strong preference for gipsy types.'

So she went to bed happy, or almost so. After all, it was all strange to her and she could hardly expect Laurens's mother to welcome her with open arms. She reminded herself that she was a foreigner.

They spent the next morning looking over the house and sitting in the garden and after lunch Laurens took himself off, declaring that he had been idle long enough and there was plenty of work which wouldn't interfere with his leg. Which left Serena sitting uncertainly in his mother's company until that lady rose gracefully, declaring her intention of calling upon an old friend. 'And you, my dear, will be glad to have an hour or so to yourself to write letters, I have no doubt.'

Serena agreed; she knew that the perfect guest always had letters to write. She fetched pen and paper and applied herself to a letter home, very colourful as to description but a little thin on news, because there really wasn't any. By the time she had finished, her hostess had gone out, driving herself, rather surprisingly, in a Mercedes, and the afternoon, barely half done, loomed emptily before her. She sat doing nothing for a little while, wishing that by some miracle, Laurens would return. But he didn't, so presently she got up and fetched her purse and set off in the direction of the town. She took the outside road because it was the only one she knew and turned into the cool dimness of the gateway's entrance, to pause there so that she could enjoy the sight of the busy little town before her. It was thronged with

people and cars, which were parked on either side
of the canal as well as in the street. She started
to walk across the little white bridge and stopped
half-way because she saw Laurens's car, parked only
a few hundred yards away. And Laurens was standing beside it, and beside him was Adriana van
Hoijden.

Serena stood still, trying to make her mind work.
Should she turn round and go away? But that
smacked of mistrusting Laurens. But if she went on
and they saw her, would it look as though she was
spying on them? As she stood trying to make up her
mind, still staring at them, Laurens bent his head
and kissed the girl standing so close to him, and at
the same moment Gijs's voice behind her said:
'What's that cousin of mine doing, kissing my girl?'

'Yours?' The relief was so great that Serena smile
brilliantly at him. 'You didn't say—I didn't
know. . .'

'I didn't realize that you were interested,' he
observed laconically. 'I asked him to tell her that I
should be a little late getting here, and look at him—
a good thing I know him well enough, and
Adriana—not to mind in the least.'

Serena put a hand on his sleeve. 'Oh, I am a fool,
aren't I?' she exclaimed happily. 'I had such a silly
idea—I actually—she's so very pretty.'

'Very—come and meet her.' He took her arm and
strolled off the bridge and on to the cobbles on the
other side, pausing several times to point out the
more interesting of the architectural features of the
houses around them. By the time she had reached
Laurens and Adriana they were standing apart, waiting for them. Before either of them could speak,
Gijs remarked placidly:

'I was just telling Serena that it was a good thing I know you so well, Laurens, or I might take exception to you kissing my girl.' He spoke deliberately and Laurens answered him a little too quickly.

'Hullo, there. Serena, how lovely to see you—if I'd known you wanted to come into town I would have come back for you instead of working. I've almost finished, though.' He didn't look at Gijs but smiled at her charmingly so that her doubts melted away. 'You two girls haven't met—Adriana—Serena,' he waved an introductory hand. 'You saw each other last night. I can't think how you missed meeting. . .'

Serena put out a small hand and shook the rather languid one offered her, and she smiled with real friendliness because this beautiful creature was Gijs's girl, not some romantic attachment of Laurens's. This must have been what Laurens meant when they were talking about Gijs on the previous afternoon. She said with pleasure: 'How nice to meet you—I've been wondering who you were.'

The girl stared at her and for a moment didn't answer, but Serena didn't notice. 'We mustn't keep you and Gijs—I hope you haven't had to wait too long.' She smiled at Laurens as she spoke and the girl said uncertainly:

'No, we didn't.'

Gijs interrupted her. 'The car's in front of the house,' he told her easily. 'We shall be late if we don't go at once.' He was staring at her very hard and Serena, seeing the look, decided that perhaps he was one of those men who hid their real feelings under a façade of laziness, because at the moment he looked curiously tense, almost anxious. But she turned away when Laurens said: 'What about tea?

I've almost finished, I can do the rest later—we'll walk back through the town, if you like.'

They split up, and as she accompanied Laurens across the street at the head of the canal she turned round to look at the others. They hadn't moved; Adriana was talking animatedly, or so it appeared from that distance, and Gijs was standing quietly, listening. Something about his attitude gave her the absurd idea that he was in a towering rage. She smiled at the thought because it was so ridiculous.

She forgot all about it during the next two days, for Laurens devoted himself to her, and his mother, while not showing any warmth towards her, at least fulfilled her duties as hostess. Serena, thinking over her days as she prepared for bed, had to admit that she had no fault to find with the older woman's manner; indeed she was fast coming to the conclusion that she was cold by nature and her rather distant treatment of herself was quite natural to her. She hadn't seen Gijs at all, and when she mentioned him idly to Laurens she was told rather shortly that he was busy with the practice. 'He's doing the lion's share at present,' he went on. 'He likes work, though you wouldn't think it to see him, would you?'

She had been there just over a week when Laurens told her that he would have to be away all day, leaving in the morning and not getting back until the evening. 'Hospital,' he said vaguely. 'Lectures and so forth, to keep us up to date, you know.'

Serena nodded. She knew all about the courses the GPs went to—it was done in England too. 'What about your patients?' she asked.

'Oh, Gijs will keep an eye on them. What will you do?'

'I don't know, but don't worry about me—I think

I'll spend a lazy day in the garden.' She missed his frown, but when she looked at him he smiled at her. 'Not worry about my gipsy girl? Don't be silly. I know! Pieter Willems—you remember meeting him the other day? he's going to Utrecht tomorrow. How about going with him? You can potter round and he'll bring you back in the evening. Mother will be out all day, it couldn't fit in better.'

'But I don't know him very well—I really don't mind. . .'

He brushed her objections aside. 'Rubbish—I insist. I'll go and telephone him now.'

So it was settled, if not to Serena's satisfaction, at least to Laurens's. She would be picked up the next morning at nine o'clock and brought home again in plenty of time for dinner in the evening.

She was having a solitary breakfast the next morning when Sieska came to tell her that there was a telephone message for her and when she went to answer it, it was Pieter who spoke. The trip was off, he explained in his careful English. His sister, with whom he lived, had developed a temperature during the night—Gijs had been and diagnosed 'flu and he didn't like to leave her—and would Serena forgive him?

She finished her breakfast and wandered aimlessly up to her room. She would have to do something with her day, Laurens had been so insistent that she should spend the day out that possibly Sieska was to have a day off as well. She went and fetched her handbag, patted her already tidy hair and went slowly downstairs; she would tell Sieska that she would be out all day. It was still only half past nine; the day stretched endlessly before her.

Gijs was in the hall. He stood relaxed as always,

with the sunlight streaming through the open door on to him, and Serena, pausing on the stairs, saw what a handsome man he was, and how elegant in his conventional grey suiting—it was funny that she hadn't noticed when they had first met, even though he had been wearing tweeds. He said without preamble:

'Hullo, you're at a loose end, I gather from Pieter. I wondered if you would like to come with me on my rounds and then have lunch? I've an hour or so to spare this afternoon, and I should like you to see my house.'

Serena advanced towards him. Just then, at that moment, she liked him very much, for in a few words he had filled the long day for her without fuss or hesitation.

'Oh, I'd like that,' she said happily. 'May I really come with you? I won't be in the way?'

'No—I daresay you will have to sit in the car for quite a time, but you can listen to the radio, or go for a stroll. I haven't many calls.'

She smiled up at him. 'I was just wondering what I was going to do with myself all day and you turned up—I'm so glad. I'm ready whenever you are.'

He turned on his heel and led her out to the Bentley and she got in beside him, feeling all at once perfectly at ease with him.

'Dreishor—you've not been there yet? Only a village, but it's built in a complete circle round a rather lovely old building which is Town Hall, school—everything, in fact. The church is interesting too. You could wander round while I see my patient.'

'There's no doctor in the village?'

'Oh, yes, but he's on holiday, so I am standing in for him.'

'But aren't you busy? Laurens isn't doing a full day's work yet, is he, and today he's had to go on this course.'

He didn't hurry with his answer and when he did it was really no answer.

'There's not much illness at this time of year,' he commented, 'there are always cases in the hospital though and a certain amount of work with the tourists. Here we are.'

The village was exactly as he had described it. She did as he had told her, strolling round the cobbled circle, viewing the church and the trees around it and the Town Hall standing in its circle of grass and flower beds. She passed the doctor's house too, and the village shops, pausing to look in their small windows, and sure enough when she reached the car again, Gijs was waiting for her.

'Coffee,' he said, and took her into the low-storied hotel which made up part of the circle of houses. It was cool and quiet inside and she would have liked to have sat over her coffee, just idly talking. Gijs—she admitted to herself that she had known it already—was an easy man to talk to. But he had other calls to make and she knew better than to hinder him. They got into the car once more and took the road to Brouwershaven and half-way there, across the flat green fields, he turned off into a lane leading to one of the farms standing well back from the road.

'I shan't be long,' he told her, and was back within five minutes. 'A post-hospital case,' he explained, 'an appendix, doing very nicely now.'

He turned the big car and went back to the road

to repeat the process several times, for most of the farms stood isolated in their fields.

'Now,' he said, 'we'll go back to Zierikzee for lunch—there's a short cut—it will take only fifteen minutes or so.'

He was as good as his word, well within that time they were going through the town gate and a moment later he slid to a gentle halt in front of the Mondragon restaurant.

They had a table by the window, and Gijs, from the attention he got, was obviously a well-known client. They talked as they ate, pleasant effortless conversation which lasted throughout the meal—Serena, later on, couldn't remember a word of it, only that it had been pleasant and restful and some-how reassuring. She had followed the chicken in Madeira sauce by a fresh fruit salad and coffee, and it was more than an hour later when Gijs suggested that she might like to see his house.

They entered through its massive front door; the hall was long and narrow with double doors on the left of them and half a dozen wide, shallow stairs on one side which ended in a wide archway, hiding, Serena guessed, the rest of the staircase. At the back of the hall was another archway, leading no doubt, to the kitchen. The floor was carpeted with a crimson carpet of great richness, soft and thick, and the walls were panelled to the plastered ceiling. The whole effect was surprisingly warm and welcoming.

'In here,' directed Gijs, and led her through the double doors into a large, high-ceilinged room, whose wide windows were curtained with apricot velvet. The floor was of highly polished wood blocks with a many-coloured carpet upon it. The furniture was a pleasing mixture of the comfortable and the antique, for the chairs were large and deep and well cushioned, upholstered in various shades of brown and apricot and peacock blue, and two or three of them were covered in needlework in a mixture of all these colours. There was a cabinet between the windows, with a brecciated marble top, its doors covered with superb marquetry, there was a Delft bowl upon it, filled with roses. Against the opposite wall was a console table, strewn with magazines, and above the great chimneypiece was a landscape, pale and vague and restful.

'What a lovely room,' breathed Serena, and her gaze went to the ceiling. 'Isn't that called strap work?'

'Yes—there's a painted ceiling in the next room.' He led the way to a door beside the fireplace. 'This is what we call a *tussen kamer*, a between room, it leads to the sitting-room beyond. Normally it doesn't have windows, but you see we have a small one. I use this room for entertaining, for it's not too large. I seldom use the drawing-room.' He smiled at her. 'I expect that when I marry, it will be used more often.'

His words gave her a curiously lost sensation which she ignored.

Later, when they had tea in the garden, lolling on the grass in the most comfortable manner and talking about nothing in particular, she looked up to surprise an expression on his face which she had never seen before, so unlike his usual placid calm that she forgot what she was about to say and asked instead: 'Why do you look like that?'

'Like what?' The look had gone—the bleak sternness she had seen; he was smiling lazily at her, his drooping lids hidings his eyes.

She said hesitatingly, still uncertain and feeling shy again and how could she feel shy with Gijs, that most comfortable of companions?—'Well, I'm not sure—angry? Did I say something to annoy you?'

'Heavens, no! I must have had a twinge of gout.'

She had to laugh then, and German the dog came and joined them where they were lying under a walnut tree and her odd, insecure moment was lost in the gentle pleasures of the afternoon.

But the feeling of shyness persisted; she had never been so aware of Gijs and he had done nothing to make her so. It bothered her, so much so that they had barely finished their tea when she declared that she would like to go back to Laurens's home, a declaration which was strengthened by the fleeting look of annoyance on Gijs's face. For some reason he didn't want her to go, but all he said was: 'Oh, come now, you can't go yet. You haven't met Lien and Jaap—they have an hour or so off each afternoon, they'll be back presently and they'll never forgive me if I let you go without meeting them.'

She was momentarily diverted. 'Oh? Then who was it brought the tea?'

'That is Wil, she comes in for a few hours a day.' He added, still persisting: 'Laurens won't be back until six at least and Tante Emilie has gone to Rosendaal, hasn't she? stay another hour or two.'

He smiled at her invitingly and she was conscious of a strong desire to remain, for she was enjoying herself; she thought a little guiltily that she hadn't meant to, not quite as much as she had done, anyway. Almost subconsciously she found herself comparing Gijs's undemanding company with Laurens, whose volatile moods she had learned to watch for and who

liked a cheerful companion who was always ready
to sparkle and laugh at everything. Gijs, she considered, would be a wonderful person to have around
if one had a headache or felt low——a disloyal idea
she doused at once, even while a voice at the back of
her mind told her clearly that even if it was disloyal it
was also true.

All the same, she got to her feet, and even the
advent of Lien and Jaap, elderly and kindly and
deeply devoted to Gijs, could not keep her for long,
and when Gijs saw that she was quite determined,
he said no more but took her outside to the car and
shut her carefully in and went round to his own seat
and got in beside her, all very slowly. He didn't
hurry back to Laurens's home either, but the journey
was so short it took barely five minutes. At the gates
she said firmly: 'Please stop here, there's no need
for you to come any further. Thank you for a simply
gorgeous day.' She smiled at him, touched him fleet-
ingly on the arm, and got out of the car.

The gates were open, so she walked through them
towards the house, turning once to wave to Gijs,
who, for some reason, had got out of the car and was
standing, doing nothing, beside it. She was almost at
the front door when she heard voices and crossed
the sanded drive to peer through the thick screen
of shrubbery which bordered the garden. Laurens
was there, so was Adriana. They were standing
together——more than together, Serena's shocked
brain registered. Adriana was in Laurens's arms and
he was kissing her, and somehow Serena knew that
this wasn't a chance meeting for them. Without
wanting to do so, she stood, her sandalled feet rooted
to the ground. There seemed no end to the kiss. She
drew a long, difficult breath and suddenly released

from her intolerable immobility, turned and flew back the way she had come, back through the gate—if only Gijs would be there!

He was. She flung herself at him and burst into tears.

CHAPTER FIVE

His arms felt comforting, but she hardly noticed that. When she had her breath again she declared savagely: 'You knew—why did you let me come back?'

If he found her question unfair he didn't remark upon it. 'If you remember,' he reminded her evenly, 'you insisted upon coming—I tried my best to make you stay.'

She swallowed tears and snatched the handkerchief he had thoughtfully offered to mop her face. 'But you know—about Laurens and Adriana—they're—they're. . .' she refused to finish the sentence. 'How long?'

When he didn't answer she banged his chest with her small clenched fist and said loudly: 'You're glad, aren't you? You never wanted me to come to Holland.'

She felt his hands on her shoulders and she was made to face him.

'You're quite wrong,' he told her gently. 'I was delighted that you came, but for all the wrong reasons. Look, you're upset. You know what we're going to do? You're coming back with me; you shall wash your face and comb your hair and I shall give you a drink, and you will sit quietly while I take evening surgery, and when that's finished I'll take you back again. You'll feel better by then—this is perhaps what you call a flash in the pan—you must give Laurens a chance to explain. I'm not qualified

107

to give advice, but if you could forget the whole thing—' His grey eyes searched hers. 'If Laurens loves you,' he went on slowly, 'everything will be all right, for everyone.'

He was right, of course. She nodded and sniffed forlornly. 'I'm sorry I said that,' she managed. 'I don't think I really knew what I was saying—you would never have been so unkind,' and then gasped as he answered pleasantly: 'Oh, but I would—I am. I didn't know that they would be there, although I imagined there might be a possibility, but since they were and you have seen them together, so much the better. Nothing is so bad if it is brought into the open.' He smiled a little, almost as though he had made a joke. 'Come along,' he said, and took her arm.

She wondered what Lien and Jaap thought when they arrived back at his house five minutes later, but she didn't really care. Lien took her upstairs to one of the lovely bedrooms and left her alone, throwing open a door to disclose a bathroom before she went. Serena, left to herself, took down her hair and washed her face and resolutely made it up again; she wasn't going to cry any more. It would probably be just as Gijs had said—a flash in the pan. When she was ready she went out on to the landing and started down the stairs, and Gij's voice called from the sitting-room: 'In here, Serena—I've five minutes before surgery.'

He barely looked at her as she went in but handed her the drink and waved her to a chair. She perched on the edge of it and took a sip, then asked, for something to say: 'I thought the surgery was in the town.'

'So it is—a couple of minutes in the car, and it

won't matter if I'm a few minutes late for once.' He smiled at her vaguely and got up to let German in from the garden. Serena, her numbed brain warmed by the sherry, asked him: 'The other afternoon on the bridge—I've just this minute remembered—you said Adriana was your girl. . .'

He stood up and set his glass on one of the tables. 'Lies, wicked lies,' he observed with calm. 'Couldn't think of anything else to say on the spur of the moment.' He was already at the door. 'I'll be back within the hour,' he told her, and was gone.

When Gijs returned he drove right up to the house and got out with her, and with a reassuring hand on her shoulder, propelled her into the house. In the ensuing greetings, explanations and exchange of the day's news Serena found it necessary to say very little; Gijs seemed to be doing it all with a casual tact she hadn't expected of him. He went away after half an hour, waving a careless hand at her but saying nothing, and she waved back, feeling utterly lost.

But that night, in bed, she realized that she had no need to feel that either, for Laurens, despite what had passed between himself and Adriana, hadn't changed in his manner towards her at all. True, he didn't know that she had seen them, but he was full of plans—vague ones, but still plans, and full, too, of pretty little compliments, the kind a girl would expect to receive from a man who loved her. Serena, her head in a complete muddle and exhausted with so much to worry about, finally went to sleep.

She saw a great deal of Laurens in the next day or so and nothing at all of Gijs. Perhaps he had been right after all and there was nothing to worry about. She wrote letters to her friends at Queen's, struggled with the headlines in the Dutch newspapers and made conversation with her hostess, and tried desperately to forget Laurens and Adriana kissing each other in the garden, and almost succeeded. It was her hostess who shattered her hard-won sense of security.

They had taken their coffee into the garden because it was such a lovely morning and Serena had painstakingly talked about all the suitable subjects she could call to mind, when her companion inquired in a gentle voice:

'And when do you leave us, Serena?'

A leading question, thought Serena, and sought for the right answer. Either her hostess was unaware that she was entertaining her future daughter-in-law, or she had set her face against her son marrying. 'Well,' began Serena, thinking hard and aware of panic beginning to knot her breath, 'I. . .'

'You see, my dear, although I have no wish to see you go, you must see for yourself that with Laurens's approaching marriage to Adriana—you did meet her, did you not?—it would hardly do for you to be here. I mean. . .'

'What exactly do you mean?' Serena's voice, by some gigantic effort on her part, was quite steady.

'Why, it would look strange, you understand? I know Laurens has been delighted to have you here— he was, and is still, so grateful for all your kindness to him in hospital, but he's a very impressionable young man,' she smiled at Serena as though they might share a little joke about this side of his character. 'But I'm sure you are a most sensible young woman.' She waited for Serena to agree and when she didn't, went on:

'You do not perhaps know that Laurens is from *adel*—Adriana also.'

'And what,' asked Serena woodenly, 'is *adel*?'

'The nobility—Laurens is a *jonkheer*. In Holland *adel* marry *adel*.' The words were said with a satisfied finality as though an undisputed fact had been stated which clinched the matter. Indeed, the speaker seemed to think that the matter had been clinched, for she went on smoothly:

'The weather has been perfect for your visit. How fortunate you have been, Serena. This warmth is really quite exceptional.'

And Serena, sick with humiliation and misery and anger, agreed in a terse little voice. She even enlarged upon the varieties of weather they had had, were having, and might expect to have in the near future. She then excused herself on the plea of letters to write and went to her room. She still felt sick, but when she looked at herself in the mirror, she looked a little pale and that was all; she had expected to see a drawn, haggard face, crisscrossed with lines of unhappiness. She re-did her face with care, for it gave her something to do and time to think. Later, when Laurens came home, she would talk to him and find out if what his mother had said was true. There was the chance that she had merely wished to discourage her from marrying him, and if Laurens really loved her, despite Adriana, it would be his chance to put things right. She had been surprised by her hostess's remarks about the nobility, but in this modern age, she argued to herself, it was surely not as important as all that.

She stayed in her room until lunchtime and arrived downstairs just as Laurens came into the house.

Before he could say anything at all, she said quickly: 'I'd like to talk to you, Laurens—now; it's

important. It won't take long—could we go
somewhere?'

He looked a little taken aback and then said readily
enough: 'In here,' and opened the sitting-room door
and ushered her in. He closed it carefully behind
him and walked towards her.

'Stay there,' said Serena sharply. 'I was told by
your mother this morning that you and Adriana are
going to be married. I just want to hear from you
that it's true, that's all. You see, I thought you were
going to marry me.' It pleased her very much that
her voice sounded so quiet and steady. She looked
at his face and knew what the answer was going to
be, for he looked, for a brief moment, ashamed at
himself, but only for a moment.

'Well, gipsy girl, it wouldn't have worked out—
us, I mean. I know I hinted, and just for a little
while. . .but I never asked you to marry me. I told
you not to fuss about that, didn't I? If I've been
thoughtless—I'm sorry, and I was going to tell you
about Adriana. . .' He smiled at her, his old, charming smile, 'No hard feelings, eh? I suppose I should
have explained, but we were having such a good
time and I suppose I didn't think you were quite so
serious—no harm done, though.'

Serena stared at him speechlessly. It seemed to
her that quite a lot of harm had been done—a broken
heart and broken pride and no job any more; she
realized then that he could never have known how
she felt about him; for him it had been a jolly little
affair, with Adriana, secure in her future, waiting
until he was ready to settle down. Serena closed her
eyes against the shame welling up inside her and
without a word went out of the room before Laurens
could do anything about it. She went out of the house

as well. She heard him calling after her as she ran through the gates. If he chose to come after her, he would have to get the car from the garage first, for it wasn't outside the door and she didn't think he would come after her. His leg prevented him, for one thing.

Zierikzee was very small and she had nowhere to go. She had slowed to a walk because people might wonder what was the matter to see her tearing down the quiet road as though the devil were after her, although there were few people about; they were all having their dinners. She had reached the Noordhavenpoort by now, and began to walk faster, because of course she had somewhere to go and someone to go to—Gijs.

Jaap let her in when she banged the brass knocker, took one look at her face and led her through the house and out into the garden. Gijs was round the corner, outside the old wing. He was sitting on an upturned bucket, in his shirtsleeves, sucking at a pipe. When he saw her, he said:

'Hullo, I rather expected you,' and then spoke to Jaap in Dutch, pulled out another bucket from the wall and added: 'Sit down, make yourself comfortable.'

She sat obediently and he followed suit, and so they remained for several minutes, with Serena fighting tears and Gijs apparently content to ponder about nothing at all with closed eyes.

'He's going to marry Adriana,' Serena told him at last in a small tight voice. 'I didn't believe his mother when she told me, but then he came home and I asked him.' Her voice wobbled alarmingly and rose a little. 'He—he—so I ran away.'

'Very sensible of you. Now take a deep breath,

dear girl, and tell me exactly what has happened.'

She did so, leaving nothing out. 'I didn't know about Laurens being a *jonkheer*—is it important? His mother said. . .'

'Not important at all, at least not in this day and age, but my aunt belongs to another generation—she sets great store upon such things.'

'Then why didn't Laurens. . .?'

He answered her with kindly patience. 'Laurens has behaved very badly—he's not a bad man, Serena, but he has a marked predilection for pretty girls. Anyone else but you. . .' He paused. 'You made a mistake, Serena—not of your own fault, let us admit, but now you must face up to it and then forget it. It will hurt at first, but not for long, that I can promise you.'

She felt the hurt bite deep into her as he spoke and a tear spilled down her cheek. 'That's right,' said Gijs comfortably, 'have a good weep—we can't talk until you have.' He put out an arm and pulled her head down on to his shoulder.

It was a great comfort to be able to cry and know that he didn't mind in the least; she sniffed and gulped and wept until she had no more tears left, and when he saw that she had at last finished, he pushed her back gently on to her bucket and got up from his own, stretched enormously, and then sat down again as though the exercise had exhausted him.

'And what are you going to do?' he inquired in the mildest of voices.

'I don't know.' She made her voice calm.

'In that case, might I suggest that you marry me?'

Serena turned her blotched face to his and gaped at him, and when she had her outraged breath again, said furiously: 'How dare you!'

'Well, yes,' he agreed placidly, 'that is something I ask myself, but I can't see anything against it, can you?'

He turned calm grey eyes to her flashing ones while she went on struggling for sufficient breath to answer him as he deserved. 'There are heaps of reasons,' she managed furiously. 'For one thing, we don't—don't. . .'

'Love each other?' he supplied with no trace of embarrassment. 'My dear Serena, how like a woman to see difficulties where there are none! We like each other—at least, I believe you have overcome your dislike of me. You need, how shall I put it? a safe anchorage, and I need someone to keep an eye on Lien and Jaap and German, and myself of course, and to help in the surgery in emergencies, listen patiently and with intelligence when I need to air my views on some knotty problem—and someone to share my table, but not, I hasten to add, my bed.'

Serena's face flamed. 'Not—not. . .' she spluttered.

'Certainly not. Oh, let me set your boggling mind at rest. I'm a perfectly normal man, but hardly an impulsive one. I should wish our marriage to be a friendly and businesslike arrangement, at least until such time as you—we—should have got to know each other really well. One might call it an engagement, only with the difference that we should be married. There would be one proviso, of course; that should you find a man you loved, you would tell me at once, so that the necessary steps could be taken.'

She opened her mouth to utter, but he lifted a languid hand. 'No, dear girl, wait until I have finished. I don't agree with easy divorce, marriage for me should be for always, but in our case I think it would hurt no one since our feelings would be untouched.'

Serena digested this in silence; presently she said slowly: 'Yes, but you—what about you? Would you tell me?'

She looked at him and saw, to her great annoyance, that he had closed his eyes, apparently exhausted by so much conversation. She raised her voice and said loudly: 'Well?'

He opened one eye. 'Dear Serena, I sowed my wild oats some time since—I'm far too busy for girls.'

'But I'm a girl.' It was ridiculous how indignant she felt.

He started to fill his pipe. 'Ah, yes—so you are, but I hardly think of you in general terms.'

She watched him light his pipe and waited for him to go on speaking, but he didn't; it seemed he had said all he intended to say. He puffed gently, his eyes half shut, which vexed her because it meant she would have to say something. 'It's a ridiculous idea,' she stated flatly and a little too loudly. 'Besides, if I lived here I should see Laurens. . .'

'So you would,' he agreed quietly. 'You would also be my wife.' He got to his feet for the second time. 'Think it over—it's not as ridiculous as it sounds.'

'Ridiculous? It's crazy—how can I bear to meet him and see him with. . .?'

For a split second the calm face above her changed to a stark, grim mask and in the same brief time was calm again. 'It won't be as bad as all that. You would have quite a busy life, you know. When you meet there will be other people there; you'll not need to see Laurens alone, unless you wish.'

'I never want to see him again,' she declared with a woman's fine logic, and burst into tears again.

Gijs pulled her gently to her feet and held her close. 'Now, now,' he spoke with firm kindliness, 'that's enough of the watering pot. We're going to have lunch and then I shall telephone Laurens and ask him to see that someone packs your things and leaves them here.'

'But I can't stay here!' She was startled out of her tears.

'Certainly not,' he agreed promptly. 'I've my reputation to consider. I shall take you to my mother.'

Serena stared at him, her mouth lamentably open again. 'Your mother? I didn't know you had one.'

'It's usual,' he remarked. 'I have a father too. I'll drive you over to their house before evening surgery and fit in my visits on the way back.'

'But I can't stay there.'

'You'll like it,' he was quite certain about that, she saw, 'and as soon as I can fix things this end I'll take you back to your home and you can meditate quietly about marrying me.'

She didn't know whether to laugh or cry again. In the end she achieved a damp smile and he said instantly: 'That's better. Come into the house, I'll pour the drinks while you effect repairs.'

He took her arm and drew her into the sitting-room through its open door, then marched her across into the hall where he shouted for Lien. Serena, waiting quietly beside him for Lien to appear, asked doubtfully:

'Did you mean all the things you said?'

'Every blessed word,' he assured her.

They lunched in the dining-room, at the back of the house and which she hadn't seen before. It was a pleasant room with windows overlooking the garden and well-polished mahogany furniture. It was a pity that Serena had no appetite at all, but she did her best and was grateful to Gijs for saying nothing about herself; instead, he talked idly about the town and the weather and the sailing which he enjoyed when he had the time, interrupting himself to say: 'I should have added crewing to my—er—needs.' He smiled so kindly at her that she wanted to cry again; instead she asked: 'How am I to tell my mother and father?'

'Why, write to them—you can do it now, while I'm arranging for your things to be sent over, and if I may I will write too. It shouldn't be too much of a shock—they have met me.'

She choked a little. 'You talk as though we were going to. . .'

'But we are, my dear, surprising though it may seem to you. When you have had time to think it over, I believe you may find the idea not unpleasant.'

'I don't know you,' she muttered miserably.

'Did you know Laurens? And you were ready to marry him. Did he ever ask you to marry him, Serena?' and when she flushed painfully, 'I shouldn't have asked that, but you have been living in a dream world of your own for several weeks; the real world won't be quite so hard, you know.' He grinned suddenly. 'I shall be a very good husband, and I do need someone to help in the surgery— my nurse is getting married shortly.'

Serena found herself laughing. 'You're ridiculous! You'll be telling me next that that's why you asked me to marry you.'

'Well, that wouldn't be quite true—I've told you my reasons for wanting to marry you—most of them anyway. I dare say we shall discover even more as we go along.'

'You won't hurry me for an answer?'

'No, but don't come over coy and wait for me to ask you again because I'm not going to. You can tell me when you're ready.' He smiled at her, 'And now write that letter while I telephone.'

Sitting beside him in the car an hour or so later, she reflected on the ease with which Gijs had seen to everything; her bags had arrived very soon after he had telephoned and if there had been a message with them he hadn't given it to her, and she didn't want to hear it. She had written her letter too, wasting a great deal of notepaper in the composing of it, and he had stowed it in his pocket to post on his way back. And now they were on their way to Renesse, where, it seemed, his parents lived. She had driven through it with Laurens and all she could remember of it was an hotel called The Pub, which they had laughed about together. The thought of that laughter almost drove her to tears again, but she held them back and asked: 'Is your father a doctor too?'

'Yes—he's more or less retired, though; he's getting on for seventy. He married rather late in life—he waited until he found the right girl.' He shot her a quick glance. 'He gives the occasional anaesthetic at the hospital and takes over the practice for me when I go away.'

'Oh, I should have thought that Laurens. . .'

'It's a large practice,' he told her gently.

They went through the pleasant little town of Renesse and out the other side, where the country was wooded and the houses, standing apart from each other, were hidden from the road. Gijs turned up a narrow lane leading towards the sea and without looking at her said:

'Don't be nervous, they're expecting us. I've told Mother that we are thinking of getting married but that it's still in the air.'

Serena clenched her hands on her handbag. 'You're being so kind,' she began, and was stopped by his easy: 'It would hardly do to show unkindness towards my future wife, would it?'

An answer she felt she should dispute because she hadn't said yet that she would marry him, but somehow she couldn't be bothered to argue, and now there was no time, for he had turned into a gateway and was driving slowly between trees along a sanded drive which presently unwound itself into a wide space before a comfortably sized house, red-tiled and gabled and not very old, and as though Serena had voiced her thought, Gijs observed: 'Not old, you see. My great-grandfather rebuilt it on the tumbledown ruins of the first one. We rarely came here while my father was in practice, but now he prefers to live here.'

They were out of the car by this time and he tucked a hand under her arm and kept it there as they went through the open front door.

The hall was surprisingly roomy with a staircase at its back with a little half landing and wings branching off each side from it. It was furnished in great good taste with a Regency wall table, two comfortable chairs upholstered in mulberry velvet and a grandfather clock. There seemed to be a great many doors leading from it, several of them half open, which made the house seem to welcome who-ever was entering it. One of these doors was thrown wide now and a small woman, no taller than Serena, darted out. She was elderly with a still pretty face and her hair, streaked with grey, was ebony black.

She began to talk before she had reached them, in a clear high voice and in English, which, while strongly accented, was readily understandable.

'Gijs, dear boy, you are here, and with the so pretty Serena—and how glad we are to welcome you to our home.' She paused and stood on tiptoe to kiss her son and then turned to Serena and kissed her cheek too.

'You do not mind if I do this? I hear of you from Gijs and I know you already,' she beamed at them both, 'and my English is not so good, but it will improve. Come inside, there is tea, and you will stop a little while, Gijs?'

'Half an hour, Mama—I can't spare more time. Where's Vader?'

'In the cellar to fetch the sherry he keeps for just such an occasion as this one.' She smiled at Serena and said with great kindness: 'It is not often that we have so lovely a visitor.'

She bustled over to the small fold-down table beside one of the easy chairs in the sitting-room, upon which a tea tray was ready, and Serena, pushed gently into a small chair covered with exquisite needlework, gave an unconscious sigh; it was all rather like being at home. The welcome had been warm and sincere, and the room, furnished with the same delicately balanced mixture of antique and comfortable as in Gijs's house, had just the same feeling of homeliness. She looked up and caught Gijs's eyes upon her and smiled at him just as the door opened and his father came into the room. It was Gijs, of course—Gijs in thirty years' time, just as tall and broad but a little heavier, with eyes just as grey and heavy-lidded, only his hair was white and his pace was slower. They even shared the same voice, she discovered, when the older man crossed the room to shake her hand and bid her welcome before going to sit with his son over their tea and enter at once into earnest conversation in their own language, leaving her to be entertained by his wife, who having poured the tea, sat down beside her, saying cheerfully: 'The men, when they are together, always it is their patients and medicine and surgery—I am married a long time, but never do I get used to this talk,' her eyes twinkled kindly. 'You are a lucky girl, Serena, that you have experience of these things so that you do not shock.'

Serena drank her tea from the fragile china cup her hostess had offered her and agreed, and her companion went on happily: 'How I shall enjoy your visit; I always wished for a daughter to talk women's talk, you know—I hope that you will stay with us for a long time.' She turned round in her chair, reminding Serena forcibly of a small brown wren because her movements were so quick and so unpredictable. 'Gijs, you do not take Serena to England at once?'

He got up and came over to her chair and put an affectionate hand on her shoulder. 'Not immediately, Mama, but in two or three days' time. I have been arranging things with Vader. And now I must go. I'll be back tomorrow, but I shall be at the hospital, so I may be delayed.'

She patted his hand. 'Come when you like, my dear. We shall take good care of Serena, of that you may be sure, only it is a pity you are not here to drink the sherry.'

He laughed softly. 'I'll have a glass tomorrow, dearest.' He bent and kissed her, smiled briefly at Serena and went away. She heard the Bentley's subdued purr as he drove away; the sound made her feel very alone.

A feeling immediately dispelled by her host and hostess who at once engaged her in conversation, plied her with more tea and then took her upstairs to a small, pretty bedroom where Doctor van Amstel put her bags down and left his wife sitting in the chair by the window, talking to Serena while she unpacked. Presently she got up, saying that dinner would be in an hour and would Serena come down when she was ready, and went away too, and Serena was alone.

Several times during that afternoon she had longed to be by herself. Now she was, and rather to her own surprise instead of brooding over Laurens she found her head full of the astonishing events of that same afternoon. She still hadn't got over the surprise of Gijs's proposal, but it now no longer seemed quite as preposterous or so absurd. She wasn't sure how it had come about, but he had been quite right when he had told her that she didn't dislike him any more—indeed, upon reflection she had to admit that she liked him quite a lot, and what was more, was quite at ease with him, just as she felt quite at ease with his parents, which considering that she had just met them, seemed extraordinary.

She changed her dress and did her hair and face, then went downstairs rather thoughtfully, to meet her host's kindly talk and her hostess's motherly preoccupation with her comfort. They drank the sherry and dined, waited upon by an elderly woman, very thin and tall, who was introduced as Maagda, and who smiled at her with great sweetness.

The rest of the evening was so like an evening in Serena's own home that she could not help but feel the comfort and security around her. There was a little conversation, the news to be watched on TV, and explained for her benefit and then discussed, the decision to give her breakfast in bed, and finally, the gentle urging to go to bed, something she had been dreading.

In her room she undressed and bathed and finally got into bed, and because she was afraid to lie in the dark and think, she sat up against the square pillows, turning the pages of a magazine someone had thoughtfully provided. She had been doing this for some ten minutes when there was a tap on the door and Gijs's mother came in.

'Not asleep,' she said with satisfaction. 'I think to myself, first Serena must talk and I shall listen and if she wishes, say nothing, and when she is empty of words, she will sleep.' She perched in a chair, folded her still pretty hands in her lap and went on, 'I think that Gijs wishes to marry you and I hope that you will marry him, but even if this is not so, if you want to tell me what happens today I will listen as a friend, you understand. That is what Gijs would wish.'

Serena had listened silently to her hostess. No wonder Gijs was such a dear with a mother like that; she was reminded forcibly of her own mother who would have offered the same brisk comfort and genuine sympathy. She had told it all to Gijs, but his mother was right, to tell it all again would be such a relief. She began without preamble, right from the very beginning.

When she had finished she asked rather forlornly:

'Does it matter so much that Laurens is—what is the word? *adel*?—or was it just an excuse?'

The little lady in the chair allowed herself a smile. 'It is important to my sister-in-law, you understand. She is, how do you say—too proud, therefore we are not such good friends. It was always the custom in Holland for those families from *adel* to marry amongst themselves, and still is, perhaps, but it is no longer so important—for me, it is of not the least importance.' She broke off to smile at Serena, 'Gijs is also *jonkheer*, as is his father.'

Serena sighed. 'Oh, dear—I didn't know. Well, that settles it. I could never marry him, it would look as though. . .'

She was halted by her hostess who fixed her with a compelling eye and declared: 'We are proud to welcome so lovely a girl into the family and with a good man of the church for a father. There could be no wife more suitable for my son.'

Serena jumped out of bed and knelt beside her hostess. It was, she felt, absolutely necessary to be honest with her, she was far too nice to pretend to. Besides, she was Gijs's mother he was nice too. 'I don't love Gijs,' she stated baldly.

To her astonishment, his mother agreed with her. 'Of course you don't—how would that be possible when you love Laurens? But love does not last unless it is cared for; it will die and you will have a whole heart again to give to Gijs.'

'But he said—he doesn't want. . .'

His mother bent forward and kissed her lightly. 'Men talk nonsense, my dear. It is for us women to know what they want. Now you will go to sleep, yes? and tomorrow is another day, Serena.'

So Serena got back into bed and her hostess bade

her good night and darted away, closing the door silently behind her. Serena, lying in the dark, listened to her feet pattering down the stairs and was asleep almost before they had died away in the hall below.

She was given no opportunity to brood in the morning; her breakfast was brought to her and she had barely finished it when Maagda came to tell her that there was a telephone call for her.

Laurens, she thought immediately—he would apologize, he would. . . All the way down to the sitting-room she rehearsed what she would say, but when she picked up the receiver, Gijs said at once: 'No, it's not, Serena. Did you sleep?'

She swallowed bitter disappointment and at the same time was happy to hear his voice. 'Yes—yes, very well, thank you. How did you know. . .?'

'Perhaps because I know you better than you know yourself.'

She murmured, 'Oh,' rather at a loss, and asked if he was busy.

'Yes. Will you tell Mother that I'll be out for dinner this evening? Enjoy your day.'

He rang off, leaving her with the feeling that she had been done out of a pleasant chat, but of course he was busy, he had said so. She went back to her room and dressed, then went downstairs again to find her host and hostess in the garden. Doctor van Amstel was grooming an elderly Alsatian, his wife was cutting roses. They stopped these occupations as she crossed the lawn to reach them and Jongvrouw van Amstel, putting down her trug, said: 'There, here is Serena, and feeling rested, I hope. We will do the flowers together and then I will show you our home and perhaps you would like to take a little walk with the doctor after the coffee, of course.'

It was nice to have her morning planned for her, Serena helped with the roses in a dim, faintly damp room at the back of the house and carried them into the sitting-room and then, after a leisurely tour of the house, sat by the open window and drank her coffee while the doctor discoursed on politics, the weather and the state of the garden. Presently he declared that he was ready to take her and Biscuit, the Alsatian, for a walk, and they set off.

Their way led through a gate at the end of the garden and along a path across the wooded land behind the dunes. They had walked in silence for a few minutes when Doctor van Amstel told her: 'Laurens telephoned this morning—he wanted to see you. I told him that I would tell you and that you would decide if you wished to see him. I hope I did right, Serena.'

She had stopped walking and stood staring at nothing. In the quiet around her she could almost hear her heart beating with painful rapidity. 'Thank you,' she managed, 'I think I'd rather not see Laurens, at least not yet.' She had a sudden splendid vision of herself, cool and gracious, and Gijs's wife, greeting Laurens with friendly charm at some party or other, and wondered if it would really be like that. But she hadn't decided yet if she would marry Gijs. She started to walk again and the doctor fell in beside her. 'A wise decision,' he commented, and following her own train of thought she said: 'You don't know me.'

'I know my son, my dear. If we turn left here there is an excellent view.'

The day passed quietly, through its hours, and Serena, fighting hurt and unhappiness, struggled through them as best she might, undoubtedly helped

by her companions, who took care not to leave her
alone to mope. Indeed, it wasn't until she was in
her room changing her cotton dress for something a
little more formal for the evening that she realized
that that was the first time she had been alone, and
although she longed to give way to her overwrought
feelings, she was bound to admit that their strategy
had worked. There was no point in crying for crying's sake; the quicker she put a cheerful face on
the future, the better. She was sitting before her
dressing table mirror, ready to go downstairs, when
there was a tap on the door, and Gijs came in. He
said Hullo in a perfectly ordinary voice and sat himself down on the window seat. 'I've arranged for us
to go to England the day after tomorrow—sorry I
couldn't manage sooner.'

Serena turned to face him. 'It doesn't matter at
all,' she assured him earnestly. 'You've been so
kind, and it's such a bother. I could go alone.'

'So you could. Would you rather do that?'

His reply had been so unexpected that she blinked
her beautiful, still puffy eyes in surprise. 'I—I—
no—that is, unless it's difficult for you? I feel very
mean, flinging myself at you like this and just letting
you arrange everything.'

He shrugged his shoulders. 'There was nothing to
arrange. Have you heard from Laurens?' His tone
was so matter-of-fact that she found herself answering him in the same vein.

'He telephoned this morning—your father
answered him. He wanted to see me, but I didn't
want to, Gijs.' She raised her eyes to his. 'Later
perhaps, if you're there.'

His face didn't lose its usual placid expression,
but she had the peculiar feeling that something had

exploded behind its calm, although his voice sounded much the same as usual. 'Just as you like. I think that would be sensible of you. Coming down? Father has that sherry waiting.'

The evening was tranquil and undemanding. Gijs stayed until almost midnight and never once did the conversation stray from the impersonal. When he eventually got up to go, Serena felt a pang of regret that she wouldn't be seeing him until he came to fetch her for their journey to England. Not wanting him to go, she asked: 'Did you write to Mother?'

'Yes, and I almost forgot, but it seemed to me as we can't leave early in the day, that we might spend the night in London—Richmond, I should say. I have an old friend living there, married to an English girl. They will be delighted to put us up.'

He didn't wait for her comments but patted her in a brotherly fashion on the shoulder, wished her the most casual of goodnights, and went out to his car.

It was inevitable that the next day the reaction should set in. The day had begun well enough, but during the morning, spent walking with her host, and the afternoon, in the garden with her hostess, the conviction that she was making an appalling mistake became firmly rooted in her mind. She should have seen Laurens at least, and given him the chance to explain. She should never have run away in such a ridiculous fashion, and certainly she should never have allowed Gijs to arrange her life for her. Perhaps even now Laurens was eating his heart out for her, too proud to see her or telephone. There was only one thing to do—she would telephone him at once. She smiled vaguely at her hostess as she got to her feet. 'May I use your telephone?' she asked in a voice which had suddenly become wobbly, and hurried into the house, oblivious of the anxious look which followed her. She actually had her hand on the receiver when Gijs said from the door: 'No, dear girl, don't do it—if you want to see Laurens, I'll take you to him.'

She jumped like a startled hare and dropped the receiver clumsily on to the table. 'Gijs—you made me jump! I didn't know you were coming. . .'

She trailed off, surprised at her feeling of guilt, and was still more surprised when he remarked blandly: 'I finished earlier than I expected at the hospital. Come along, we'll go now.'

'No, I don't think. . .' She was all at once perverse. 'Yes.'

He hadn't raised his voice, nor had he sounded angry, but she followed him silently from the room and out of the house to where the Bentley stood at the front door.

He drove silently and very fast, it seemed only a matter of moments before he was parking the car in front of the Mondragon. It was as she was getting out that she saw, too late, the Jag.

'I won't!' she said fiercely. 'You can't make me.'

He didn't bother to answer her but tucked a hand under her elbow and steered her across the cobbles and into the restaurant. He paused in the doorway and looked round the room; it was only half full and at one of the tables near the windows were Laurens and Adriana. Serena could have killed him when he raised a hand in a casual wave and murmured lazily:

'Well, well, see who's here!' So she waved and smiled too, her eyes glittering with rage and her colour high so that she looked truly magnificent.

'I hate you!' she whispered, and smiled once more

as they were led to a table on the other side of the restaurant. When they were seated, she with her back to Laurens and Adriana, she repeated: 'Did you hear me? I hate you!'

'And very naturally. A healthy sign, too, dear girl. What would you like to drink? Something cooling, perhaps—Dubonnet with ice?'

He gave the order and sat back in his chair with such a relaxed air that Serena thought that he was about to go to sleep. 'I see,' he murmured, 'that I am to be cast in the role of enemy.' He cocked an inquiring eyebrow at her. 'Dear enemy, I hope?'

Despite his lazy air his eyes were very alert. She was suddenly full of remorse. 'What a beast I am!' she burst out. 'Gijs, I'm sorry. Why do you bother with me? I've made such a fool of myself. . .' she faltered. 'I don't think—that is, are you sure?'

'You asked me that before, dear girl. I can but repeat myself. Yes.'

'But supposing I don't—and you take me home and I. . .?'

'What you want to know is do I intend to black-mail you into marrying me by taking you back to England, thus making it necessary for you to be grateful. Tut-tut, Serena, that is bird-witted of you—don't you recognize a friend when you meet one?'

It was fortunate that the Dubonnet arrived at that moment, for she was on the verge of tears, and this time they weren't tears for herself, but for Gijs because she had been so beastly to him; good-natured, easy-going Gijs who was proving a tower of strength. She smiled mistily at him and said: 'Gijs, you are a dear,' and then, when a sudden memory came unbidden into her head: 'When you fetched me from hospital and took me home, was it Laurens? It was you, wasn't it? And the second time too—and the flowers.' She closed her eyes for a moment because otherwise she would have burst into tears; all this time she had thought it was Laurens thinking of her and it had been Gijs being kind and thoughtful. She opened them and said steadily: 'You were so kind.'

'Dear girl, let us not exaggerate my good intentions. Drink up, you'll need a little of our famous courage, I think. They're coming over.'

They came. Serena, a little white and wooden as to voice, smiled and nodded and murmured nothings while Gijs, by some miracle, contrived things so well that after the first greeting, she didn't have to speak to Laurens at all. They went at last and Gijs said at once: 'Now we'll have dinner, shall we? I'll just ring Mother not to expect us for a couple of hours.'

He strolled off, leaving Serena cold and empty of feeling except for a childish terror that Laurens would come back while Gijs was away. When he came back after what seemed an aeon of time, the sight of him warmed the cold inside her, it was like coming out of a cold mist into the sunshine. She would have liked to have told him that, but she felt sure that he would only laugh at such sentimental nonsense.

She thanked him warmly when they got back to Renesse. 'I want to talk to you,' she told him. 'There's such a lot I want to say.'

'All the time in the world to talk. Go to bed now; I'll be here at three o'clock tomorrow—and mind you're ready. I'm not allowing much time.'

She said good night a little shyly, was wished *wel te rusten* by his parents, and went upstairs to bed, where she fell asleep almost immediately, before she had had time to think anything at all.

CHAPTER SIX

THEY left the following afternoon, speeded on their way by a warm farewell from the doctor and his wife, with Maagda and the odd job man fulfilling the office of Greek chorus. Gijs's mother had kissed Serena when she had said goodbye. 'Come back soon,' she had said. 'There will be a welcome for you, my dear—and take care of Gijs.'

This remark had stuck persistently in Serena's mind ever since, popping out from time to time throughout their journey. The idea of Gijs needing anyone to look after him had never entered her head; he had seemed self-sufficient enough and perfectly able to cope with any situation which night arise, a theory largely due to his size and calm air, she had no doubt. Perhaps his mother was nervous of his driving, but although he drove fast he was a good driver and rarely put out; even in the Mini he had shown no signs of impatience. She remembered how she had sat beside him, wishing they could go faster so that she could be back at Queen's and see Laurens again. . .it seemed a long time ago.

'If I say a penny for them, I should only be teasing you and myself as well,' observed Gijs, breaking the long silence between them. 'We're up to time, with luck we shall be in Richmond by midnight.'

He was right; the journey was uneventful and Serena enjoyed it. Gijs was good company; he had given her a meal on board and accompanied her to the ship's shop to purchase whisky for her father and perfume for her mother, and then, because she had refused his offer of a cabin in which to rest, they had gone on deck and walked around and Gijs talked just sufficiently to keep her mind off her own thoughts.

They had got away quickly from the ferry, too, out of the quiet town and on to the A20 and the motorway, the big car moving without effort through the not quite dark of the summer's night. Presently he switched on to the A205, to circle the south of London and then turned off again for Richmond.

'You've been here before,' Serena hazarded.

'Yes, I stayed here when I came over to see Laurens—and at other times before then. Hugo's older than I, but we both went to the same medical school.' He turned his head to look at her in the gloom. 'Nervous?'

'Yes.' She felt his hand clasp hers momentarily. 'Don't be, they're nice.'

'Do they know about—about me?'

'If you mean about Laurens, no. They know that you have been staying with my people and that I'm driving you home—they also know that you're someone special.'

Serena felt her heart jerk at his words. 'But I haven't. . .'

He sounded very matter-of-fact. 'That makes no difference, Serena, you'll always be someone special, whether you marry me or not.'

'Why?' She tried to see his face and couldn't, but she saw him shrug.

'Oh—I suppose I like you more than most people I know.' He sounded off-hand and she was aware that her feelings were hurt, which, seeing that she had no feelings for anyone else but Laurens, was absurd. She opened her mouth, determined to pursue the subject, when Gijs said laconically:

'Here we are.'

He turned the car into a short private road close to the river, where there were several Georgian bow-fronted houses, as remote from the busy streets around them as they must have been when they were first built.

Gijs stopped at its end in front of a house with an oblique view of the river and got out. He didn't speak as he opened the door and helped Serena out, but she was grateful for the hand he tucked under her elbow; he had said that they were nice people, but they might ask questions and to answer them would be painful. But he gave her no time to hesitate and as they reached the door it was opened. The man standing there was as tall and broad as Gijs, but his hair was grey above a handsome face; it was a kind face too, and when Gijs said: 'Hullo, Hugo, this is Serena,' he took her hand and said: 'We're delighted that you have come, Serena—come in. Sarah is in the kitchen making the coffee.'

The house was as gracious inside as she had expected it would be. Serena had only a moment to look around her before the doctor's wife came in. She was a beautiful young woman with burnished hair and enormous eyes. 'I knew that the moment I went to the kitchen you would arrive,' she remarked serenely, and went straight to Serena. 'I'm Sarah, and it's lovely to have you.' She smiled with great sweetness, kissed Gijs and said, 'Hullo, Gijs,' then still smiling, but this time at her husband: 'Hugo dear, will you fetch the tray—it's all ready.' Her husband disappeared kitchenwards and his wife urged Serena to sit down and then sat down beside her. 'Did you have a good trip?' she wanted to know. 'We're going over in a month or six weeks.'

'With the twins?' asked Gijs.

'Of course. They'll be one, you know, and we thought it would be rather super if they had their first birthday in Holland.' She turned to Serena. 'One of each,' she explained happily, 'such a good start, don't you think? I'm almost thirty, you see.'

'Twins must be fun,' said Serena, and meant it. 'What do you call them?'

'The boy's Hugo, of course, the girl's called Rosemary.' She looked at her husband as she spoke and he put down the tray he was carrying and said smilingly: 'For a very special reason, but the next daughter will be called Sarah.'

'Ah, yes—Rosemary for remembrance,' said Gijs softly, 'I can't say that parenthood has taken its toll of either of you—you both look as though you've just left church, covered in confetti. How's the practice, Hugo?'

Sarah glanced at Serena and laughed. 'Here we go,' she said, 'bones and bodies!' She paused to pour the coffee. 'What do you think of Holland?'

'Well, what I saw of it I liked very much. I— we didn't go anywhere very much, but I thought Zierikzee was delightful. I should like to be there in the winter.'

Sarah gave her a considered look but didn't make any comment. 'Hugo's family live in the Veluwe— we go over fairly often. My people live near Salisbury—you're from Dorset, aren't you?'

They talked together happily until Gijs got to his feet saying that he had better put the car away and Hugo elected to go with him.

'Then I'll show Serena her room,' said his wife,

'and you two can lock up—and don't stay up talking too late, darling.'

Her husband gave her an amused, fond glance. 'No, my love. Good night, Serena, sleep well.'

She wished him good night and Gijs too, and was instantly vexed at his casual 'Sleep well.'

He could at least have—have what? she asked herself. Why should he treat her in any way but the most casual? He didn't know if she was going to say yes or no, did he? She followed her hostess upstairs into a charming room with a little iron balcony overlooking the back garden.

Sarah sat down on the bed. 'This used to be my room—it's nice, isn't it?' and went on, as if in answer to Serena's look of inquiry: 'When I married Hugo I was in love with someone else, or at least, I thought I was.' She smiled. 'It didn't take me long to discover that it was Hugo all the time—so silly.' She got up and wandered across the room. 'The bathroom's through there. Gijs's room is on the other side of the landing and we're in the front.'

'Where are the twins?' Serena was peering into the bathroom with admiring interest.

Their mother beamed at her. 'Would you like to see them? We're both so crazy about them that we're apt to forget that some people aren't too keen on babies.'

She led the way across the landing and through a large baize-lined door.

'We've a marvellous nanny—a niece of Hugo's nanny, actually—she looks after the babies and us too.' She grinned disarmingly and led the way into the nursery where Serena and she spent several minutes peering at the small creatures in their cots.

'Hugo's very like Hugo,' commented Serena.

Sarah nodded. 'I couldn't have borne it if he wasn't.'

Serena glanced at her companion. The van Elvens must love each other very much. 'I expect Hugo thinks the same about the little girl,' she suggested, and felt a pang of envy.

She was awakened in the morning by a variety of sounds small voices, mingling with the doctor's deep one and Sarah's gentle laugh: there were dogs barking too and once, a cat's miaouw. She wondered about getting up and was on the point of doing so when there was a tap on the door and an elderly woman came in with tea. She put the tray down on the bedside table and said cheerfully: 'Good morning, Miss Potts. I'm Alice, the housekeeper. Mrs van Elven asked me to tell you that breakfast is in half an hour, but if you like to have it in bed, you've only got to say so.'

Serena sat up. 'Oh, no, I'd like to come down.'

Alice smiled nicely and went away, and Serena sipped her tea, then dressed rapidly and went downstairs. There was no one in the sitting-room and she didn't know where the dining-room was. She was about to try one of the other doors in the hall when Gijs came in from the garden.

'Hullo,' he said cheerfully. 'Come into the garden. Hugo and Sarah won't be long. They always have a walk together before breakfast, nothing stops that. Did you sleep?'

'Yes, thanks. Gijs, you were right, they're very nice people.'

A moment later Sarah and Hugo appeared.

'Breakfast with the children, if you can bear it,' Sarah explained gaily, 'otherwise Hugo doesn't see enough of them. They're pretty awful feeders, I'm afraid, but Gijs doesn't mind—I hope you won't either.'

The meal was a cheerful affair; the twins chumped their way through egg and fingers of bread and butter and great draughts of milk and then, their faces wiped clean, went to sit on their father's knees while he finished, quite unperturbed, his own breakfast. Serena sighed without knowing it and looked across the table at Gijs to find that for once his eyes were wide open, staring at her.

They left soon after breakfast, after the doctor had gone and after another cup of coffee and a gossip with Sarah and a final look at the twins. And when they went, Sarah said 'We shall see you again, Serena—this visit was far too short,' but to Gijs she expressed the hope that he wouldn't be late for dinner that evening as she kissed him good-bye. 'Hugo's got some interesting theory about something or other for one of his patients, I can't remember exactly what it is, but I'm sure you'll be wildly interested.' She grinned at him cheerfully.

They were barely out of sight of the house when Serena unable to restrain her tongue for a moment longer, demanded: 'You're coming back here tonight?'

Gijs slid the car into the stream of traffic. 'Yes.'

'But I thought—that is, I expected that you would stay the night at home.'

'You didn't invite me, dear girl.' He answered her without rancour.

'Gijs, I never meant not to, I just didn't think. What beast I am! Will you stay?' It suddenly became most important that he should. 'You could ring up Sarah.'

'I have to get back—the practice, you know.'

She knew it was an excuse; his father was taking
the practice for him, another day wouldn't have mattered, but she had deserved it. She agreed with him
with an unexpected meekness and he began immediately to talk about something else.

They had coffee in Winchester, in the Close with
the cathedral close by, and Gijs discussed architec-
ture and gave her no opportunity to ask any more
questions of a personal nature, but later, when they
were streaking along the A31 towards Dorchester,
she asked: 'Gijs, have you ever been in love?'

If he was surprised there was no sign of it on his
face. He answered on a laugh. 'Oh, dozens of times,
though I can't remember them all—there was one
glorious redhead. . .'

Serena found herself taking immediate exception
to the redhead. 'I'm not interested in what they
looked like,' she snapped tartly. She didn't look at
him, so that she missed the gleam in his eyes.

He was suddenly smooth. 'Why should you, dear
girl? I wonder why you asked?'

Although he had asked the question he didn't
sound in the least interested in getting an answer,
which made it difficult for her to say: 'Well, I
thought we ought to know more about each other.'

'A moot point and one upon you may rest assured.
What did you think of the twins?'

Such a change of topic was impossible to ignore,
so she answered coldly, feeling deflated; he had so
obviously not wanted to talk about themselves.

It was just after one o'clock when they arrived at
the Rectory, and this time there was no one at the
open door, only her mother calling to them from the
kitchen that they were to go straight in. Serena ran
down the hall and across the uneven brick floor to

where her mother stood at the stove. It was lovely
to see her again; she embraced her warmly and her
mother said: 'Darling, how lovely to see you—
dinner's just ready. Run up the garden and tell your
father, he's picking peas.'

Gijs had come in too, and Mrs Potts held out two
rather floury hands. 'Gijs, we can never thank you
enough.'

He smiled a little. 'You had my letter, Mrs Potts?'

'Yes—we both read it.' Her eyes searched his
placid face a little anxiously. 'You're sure?'

'Of myself? Yes. Of Serena? Sure enough to take
a bet on it.' He took her two hands between his own,
flour and all, and gave them a reassuring shake and
she smiled a little uncertainly at him.

'I couldn't wish for anything else—I never met
Laurens, but I felt. . .' she paused. 'Serena has so
much love to give and we were so afraid that she
had given it to the wrong man. She's inclined to
give with both hands.'

Gijs's nice firm mouth quivered ever so slightly.
'I know—will you trust me?' And when she nodded,
'I'll fetch Serena's luggage.'

He was at the door and Serena and her father were
coming in from the garden when Mrs Potts said: 'Of
course you're staying the night, Gijs.'

Serena stood very still, looking at him, hoping
very much that he would say yes, but he refused,
very nicely, and she said nothing while her mother
voiced her protests, although she couldn't resist giving him an imploring look as he turned away—a
look which he blandly ignored. She took care not to
look at him again and although she chattered with
brittle gaiety throughout their meal, she didn't
address him once.

It wasn't until after dinner, when he was getting into the car for the return trip to Richmond, that the dreamlike state she had been living in was swept away by the realization that he was actually going away—just like that—without a word as to when she would see him again. She wouldn't see him again; she ran across to the car and laid an urgent hand on the door, saying frantically: 'Gijs, you can't go!'

'You don't want me to go?'

'No—I've just thought, if you go now, I'll never see you again.'

'Quite right, dear girl.'

'Oh, Gijs, if you still want me, I'll marry you. I don't love you, you know that, but I like you so much—more than anyone else I know—and I'm happy with you, if you think that's enough. I can't imagine you not being there.'

He switched off the engine then. 'A little talk, my dear? Somewhere quiet—the kitchen garden, perhaps.'

He got out of the car and they walked round the side of the house and through the narrow wooden gate leading to the walled garden where her father grew his vegetables and fruit. It was quiet there and completely shielded from the house. Half-way down the path bordering the neat rows of beans and onions and peas, he stopped.

Serena didn't know what she had expected him to say, so she was wholly surprised when he remarked: 'A white wedding, Serena, don't you agree? Here, naturally, and soon. All our relatives and friends—bridesmaids. . .'

She gasped at him. 'But I thought that you would want a very quiet wedding.'

'Why?' She saw his mouth twitch with amusement.

'I thought—it's not quite. . .' She stopped, frowning, because it was almost impossible to put into words what she wanted to say and she had the impression that he knew quite well and didn't intend to help her.

'Wrong, Serena. A wedding should be a happy occasion, and we intend to be happy, do we not? Not perhaps in the sense that most newly married couples are happy, but happy nevertheless. Besides, you will look very lovely in a white dress and a veil and all the other bits and pieces brides wear.'

'Yes?' she asked faintly. Put that way it seemed so sensible. 'Well, if you would like that.' She smiled at him doubtfully and he bent and kissed her gently on her cheek which somehow reassured her, as did his: 'Trust me, Serena, you'll have your doubts and fears, but I promise you they will mean nothing.'

Of course she trusted him, and said so, quite surprised that he should ask such a thing of her, suddenly content to let him decide everything for her. It was all the more disappointing, therefore, when he looked at his watch. 'I must go.'

'Please stay, Gijs—couldn't you possibly?'

He smiled lazily at her. 'No, my dear, but do you suppose that I could have five minutes with your father before I leave? The banns and so forth. How about a month's time for the wedding—there is no reason why we should wait. I'll be over again very shortly. Don't worry about notices in the papers and so forth, I'll see to all that—just concentrate on being a beautiful bride.'

She nodded wordlessly and they walked back to

the house together and found her mother and father
sitting together Serena said baldly: 'Mother, Father,
Gijs and I are going to get married, and Gijs wants
to talk to you, Father.'

It was later, long after Gijs had gone and she had
unpacked and had supper and gone to bed after an
excited family discussion about her future, that she
remembered that her parents hadn't seemed in the
least surprised at her announcement, nor had Laurens
been mentioned. She would, she decided as she got
into bed, talk to her mother in the morning and try
to explain.

Her opportunity to do this came soon after breakfast, with Susan dispatched on some errand or other,
her father closeted in his study and her mother
embarked on bedmaking.

Serena mitred her corner with unnecessary care
and began: 'Mother, about Laurens—I've been an
awful fool.'

Her mother thumped a pillow. 'No, dear, you
would have been a fool if you had gone on with it
and tried to alter something which couldn't be
altered, and married him. It hurts now, but it would
have hurt much more if you had married.'

Serena finished her side of the bed and sat down
on it. 'It hurts now, Mother, and I can't think straight.
I don't even know why I'm going to marry Gijs—
does that shock you? I like him more than anyone
I know—I like him more than Laurens, isn't that
strange? but I don't love him. How can I when I
love Laurens? And Gijs is so sure that it will be all
right—he doesn't love me, you know. He wants a—
a companion, someone to run his home and help
him sometimes in the surgery and listen to him—

oh, Mother, is it wrong of us to marry, not loving each other?'

Her mother gave her a loving look which she didn't see, nor did Serena see the expression on her mother's face—that of a small child with a secret she longed to share and mustn't. She came and sat beside Serena.

'No, love. And if your father had thought that he would have said so, even though you are quite old enough to do what you like with your life.' She got up off the bed. 'If any man can make you happy, it's Gijs,' she said positively.

'I didn't like him very much when we met.'

Her mother paused on her way to the door. 'My dear child, I loathed your father for quite some time before I fell in love with him.'

Serena contemplated her parent with open-mouthed astonishment. 'Mother, darling. . .'

'Yes, and don't you tell your brothers and sisters. I'm only telling you so that you realize that yours is by no means an isolated case.'

A week went by, during which Serena received a copy of the *Telegraph* with the announcement of their engagement in it, and another copy of *Elseviers Weekblad* from Holland with the same announcement, in Dutch, of course, but there was no word from Gijs, although his mother and father wrote; warm letters expressing their delight at the prospect of having her for a daughter-in-law. There was a stiffly worded note from Laurens's mother, but there was nothing from Laurens, and her disappointment was almost equalled by the sense of relief that he hadn't written. Sarah and Hugo wrote too, a warm, friendly letter; so did her friends at Queen's, all anxious to know when the wedding was to be something which she couldn't tell them because she didn't know herself.

It was on the Saturday morning, as Serena came in from the garden with a basket of flowers, that she found Gijs standing in the hall with her father, chatting with the air of someone who had just dropped in for a casual ten minutes. She went towards him, foolishly put out because he hadn't come into the garden to find her, and even now, when he saw her, his greeting was markedly matter-of-fact and his cheerful 'Hullo, Serena!' did nothing to arouse her feelings, nor did the quick conventional kiss on her cheek. Still, she told herself sensibly, she didn't want it otherwise, did she, and neither did he, so why was she allowing such a trifle to upset her?

'You're staying, of course,' stated Mrs Potts, who had come downstairs to join them.

'You're very kind. If I may—I must be back on Monday, but that will give Serena and me time to discuss several things. Besides, I have to hear these banns read.'

'Very right and proper,' observed Mr Potts. 'And now if you'll excuse me, I must finish my sermon.'

'Take Gijs into the garden,' commanded Mrs Potts, 'and I'll make coffee presently.' She nodded in a satisfied way and started back upstairs again.

'But, Mother—the beds.'

'Blow the beds,' declared Mrs Potts inelegantly, and disappeared on to the landing above.

Serena glanced at Gijs and found him faintly smiling. He took the basket from her, set it on the hall table, then suggested: 'The garden, then, since your mother suggests it.'

'I didn't know you were coming.' Serena knew

that she sounded grumpy as she spoke, but she felt so; it was annoying that she should be wearing an elderly cotton frock of a rather well-washed blue because she had intended to do some gardening. She hadn't bothered with her hair either, and it hung down her back, tied back with a ribbon.

He took her arm. 'No time to write,' he explained, 'and I was afraid to telephone.'

She stopped to look up at him. 'Afraid? Whatever for?'

'You might have changed your mind.'

She was shocked. 'But I promised.'

He didn't answer her, only bent his head and kissed her gently on the mouth, then took her arm again and went on walking. 'How many bridesmaids?' he asked.

'Well, none so far.' Really, he was the most vexing man, and so unpredictable! 'How could I ask anyone when I don't even know when we're going to be married?'

'Don't brides choose their wedding day? Let us see, the earliest date would be three weeks from Sunday, that's tomorrow—the Monday?'

She found herself laughing. 'Yes, all right. There's hardly time to send out the invitations, though. And they're not even printed.'

'We'll go to Dorchester this afternoon and see about that, and you can let the bridesmaids know—and buy your wedding dress if you wish.'

'Gijs, I couldn't possibly, not just like that. I can see about the bridesmaids—Susan, of course, and I thought I'd ask Joan—from Queen's, remember? But I can't buy my dress today—I think I'll have it made. . .'

She gazed into nothing, momentarily diverted by

a beautiful vision in white—her mother's veil, naturally, and would Susan look her best in pink—and
Joan? She repeated firmly: 'I couldn't.'

Gijs had stopped again. 'I almost forgot,' he said,
plunged his hand into a pocket and took out a little
leather box and opened it. There was a ring inside,
three rubies encircled with diamonds and set in an
old-fashioned gold band. 'I hope it fits,' he said,
and picked up her hand and slipped it on. 'It's my
grandmother's betrothal ring—there are two in the
family—Mother has one, this is the other.'

She held it up to the sunlight and watched the
gems sparkling. 'It's very beautiful, Gijs, I've never
had anything so lovely before. Are—are you sure
you want me to have it?'

His nice mouth quirked a little at its corners.
'Quite sure, dear girl, and if you have any more
doubts, shall we have them now and settle them
once and for all?'

Serena stared up at him. 'Haven't you any?' she
demanded, and when he shook his head, she went
on: 'I've one or two, yes. Gijs, I didn't know that
you were a *jonkheer*—I asked your mother about it
and she said it didn't matter—not to her—but what
about you? L-Laurens's mother minded very much,
she seemed to think that—Father's middle class, you
know,' and then added hastily in case he should
misunderstand: 'Not that I'm ashamed of that.' She
drew a little breath. 'He's. . .'

'A very learned man—and a good and wise one,'
Gijs finished for her, 'and since we are letting down
our metaphorical back hair, there is something else:
I have a good deal of money, Serena, something
which I find relatively unimportant in my life. I
would hope that you will regard it in the same light.'

'Well, I'll try, though I think I may have to get used to it.'

'I'll be there to help you. Straight back to work after the wedding, Serena—will you mind?'

'No, I shan't mind. The quicker I get used to being a Dutch housewife the better.' They were standing at the end of the garden, facing each other, and she reached up and kissed his cheek. 'Thank you for my lovely ring, Gijs—I'll try and live up to it.'

'And that's another thing. We had better shop around for a wedding ring.'

'Yes—and one for you?'

The sleepy grey eyes were all at once bright and intent. 'You like the idea?'

'Yes, of course—don't you?'

'Yes. Isn't that your mother calling?'

The weekend was a dream in which Serena knew herself to be living, and like all dreams, nothing that she or anyone else said or did seemed in the least strange, which was probably why, when Gijs left to return to Holland on Sunday evening, she kissed him goodbye with a fervour which, while entirely to be expected in a loving bride-to-be, was hardly called for in her case.

She hadn't a minute to call her own during the next weeks, still less time to think deeply about anything. Even a small country wedding, it seemed, needed a terrific amount of planning and organizing. She wrote invitations, shopped for clothes, spending her savings lavishly, and had her wedding dress fitted, and because Gijs couldn't spare the time to come to England again before the wedding, she wrote to him regularly. Not that he answered her letters, she hadn't expected him to, but he did telephone her almost every day. She looked forward to his calls more than anything else, and on the rare occasions when he did not do so, she moped round the house and went early to bed, a little cross.

It seemed hardly possible that she should wake one morning and know that the very next day was her wedding day and that Gijs would be with her within a few hours. He was travelling alone, ahead of his family, all of whom would stay in Dorchester and drive over for the wedding, but Gijs with Hugo van Elven, who was to be his best man, and of course, Sarah, were putting up at Cerne Abbas and he would be coming over to the Rectory that evening. To Serena the day seemed endless, with last-minute arrangements to make, the flowers to do in the church, lengthy discussions with Susan over the best hairstyle to adopt and Margery waylaying her as often as she could, in order to tell her, over and over again, how marvellous being married would be. They had just sat down to tea when Gijs came in with a casual, 'Hullo, everyone,' and a light kiss for her as he joined them. As he sat down beside her, Serena said: 'I didn't expect you just yet—did you get an earlier boat?'

'No—a Hoverlloyd—very quick, a bit further to drive on the other side, but that's no problem.' He gave her a bright glance and then dropped his lids. 'Are you ready?'

She passed him his tea and offered him the scones she had had time to make earlier in the day. 'I think so—there's been so much to do, but I don't think we've forgotten anything.'

For the rest of the evening Serena wasn't alone with him at all, and his brief goodnight was cool and friendly. She went upstairs to bed, a prey to a hotchpotch of thoughts while admitting to herself that it was a little late to try and sort them out.

The morning was brilliant. The wedding was to be at the early hour of ten o'clock, for Gijs planned to leave at half past one in order to catch the evening ferry, and even then he was cutting it a little fine. Serena indulged with the time honoured custom of breakfast in bed, entertained a constant stream of visitors to her room.

Alone at last, she began the business of bathing and dressing; she had finally decided on a dress of cream silk with long tight sleeves and a high round neck; its simple lines suited her slim figure and showed off her dark beauty to its greatest advantage. She had done her hair in its usual simple bun on top of her head. Now with Susan's doubtful help and Joan and Margery as audience, she arranged the veil, its wreath of orange blossom encircling the bun, its soft folds framing her face and shoulders. She looked quite nice, she admitted to herself as she stood before the mirror, although she was perhaps a little too pale—she turned to face her mother as she came into the room.

Being married, she told herself as she walked down the aisle on Uncle William's arm, with her father waiting for her at the other end, and only Gijs's broad back to pin her gaze to, was like a dream; she knew she was the bride, but it didn't seem quite real; she couldn't believe that in ten minutes she and Gijs would be man and wife. She would have liked to look around her as they made their slow way, but brides didn't look around them, not as they came into the church. She could do that presently, as they came out again, only then she would be holding a different arm.

It seemed no time at all before they were walking

out of the church again. She hardly remembered the service or the kiss they had exchanged in the vestry; she had certainly heard no word of her father's little homily to them both. Now, her hand on his arm, she did look around her, smiling a little shyly at Gijs's family and friends, looking quickly past Laurens and over to the other side of the aisle where her own family were. They paused in the porch for the photographs, then walked across to the Rectory, where the sexton's wife and the postman's daughter were waiting in their best dresses to hand round the tit-bits her mother had ordered from Dorchester. The postman was there too, to serve the drinks and open bottles under the rector's mild direction; they smiled their good wishes as Serena and Gijs crossed the hall and went into the drawing-room, seldom used because it was too large and draughty, but on such an occasion as this one, a blessing in disguise, for it could hold fifty people with ease, and to make even more space the doors on to the garden had been flung open. Through them Serena could see the guests breaking up into small groups and start to make their way towards the house.

She hadn't been aware that she had been holding Gijs's hand, but now that he took it away, she was, and she put out her own hand again in mute appeal.

'Just a moment, my dear,' his voice was quiet as she felt his fingers at her neck. 'My wedding present, Serena,' he said, and kissed her before turning to smile at her parents and his own mother and father who had come to join them.

Serena put up a quick hand and felt. Pearls— they felt soft as silk between her fingers. She whispered, 'Thank you, Gijs,' and slipped her hand back in his, feeling his reassuring squeeze as the first of the guests came through the door.

She remembered reading once some novel or other in which the dim-witted heroine had declared on the last page that the hero was like a calm harbour after the stormy seas through which she had been struggling. Serena had thought at the time that the metaphor had been a singularly clumsy one—no man would care to be likened to a harbour; now she wasn't so sure, for she herself felt exactly as the tiresome girl in the novel had felt and Gijs, although not in the least like a harbour, had all its qualities. And now deep within her, she felt a faint warm glow in place of the stony misery she had been carrying around with her since the day she had gone to Gijs for help. She hardly recognized it, only, standing there beside him, she felt the beginnings of happiness.

CHAPTER SEVEN

THE glow was still there as she waved goodbye to everyone from the Bentley as Gijs drove away from the Rectory an hour or so later. Her head was filled with a kaleidoscope of sound and colour, people and voices, church music and wedding cake and, not least of all, Gijs putting the ring on her finger and promising to cherish her for the rest of his life. She twiddled the wedding ring on her finger and, anxious to appear at ease, asked: 'I hope you enjoyed the wedding, Gijs?' and saw the corner of his mouth lift in a smile.

'Indeed I did, my dear—I had no idea that being married was so enjoyable a process.' He shot her a quick sidelong glance. 'And the bride more than fulfilled my expectations—you were beautiful, Serena.'

'Oh—was I? I'm glad you liked me. I thought you looked pretty trendy yourself.' She put a hand up to the pearls at her throat. 'I haven't thanked you properly for these yet—they're fabulous.'

He pulled into the side of the road and stopped the car. 'Do thank me properly,' he begged, and turned to her, a wicked gleam in his eyes.

Serena was conscious of her heart racing and then a sense of disappointment when he added, 'Between friends, of course.' She leaned up and kissed him, telling herself that to feel disappointment was absurd; it wasn't as if they were in love—was she not in love with Laurens? And Gijs? He, apparently, wasn't in love with anyone, so why should she suddenly remember Adriana?

'Not bad—not bad at all for a wifely kiss. I daresay you will get more experienced as the years roll by.'

She drew back a little so that she might see his face. She said indignantly: 'Well, really, you talk as though I'm the one who's going to do all—all the kissing!'

'Ah, but I don't need any practice.' She felt his arm pull her close as he kissed her; an entirely different affair from the short, light salute she had accorded him; indeed, he kissed her several times so that she became a little breathless and her cheeks pinkened delightfully, and when he at last loosed her anything she had intended to say had flown out of her head.

Then he glanced at his watch and with a casual remark to the effect that they had no more time to waste, sent the car ahead at a great rate, leaving her to brood over the fact that he had considered the little interlude a waste of time.

They had a late tea on board, although the restaurant was on the point of serving evening grills. Serena, watching a steward clearing a table and relaying it for them, wondered how big a tip Gijs had given him. It would be strange not to have to worry about such things any more; she supposed that she would get used to it.

They were the first off at Zeebrugge and quickly took the lead from the other cars, for Gijs was racing to catch the ferry at Breskens. Once clear of that and on the other side of the river, he didn't slacken speed but tore on along the main road towards Goes and then over the three-mile-long bridge connecting the islands, and finally, Zierikzee.

They had made good time; it was still before midnight as he dawdled the big car carefully through the gateway and into the Oudehaven. It was almost in darkness. Across the canal the restaurant was still open and the street lamps cast their reflections in the water. Gijs's own house was lighted, the great square windows glowed as he drew up before the massive front door, thrown open at once to reveal Jaap and Lien, smiling broadly. Serena sat uncertainly until Gijs said: 'Home, Serena' in such a quiet voice she scarcely heard him as he helped her out.

Inside the house welcomed them; there were flowers everywhere, a delicious smell seeping from the kitchen, and Lien and Jaap both talking at once, shaking first her hand and then Gijs's. Presently Jaap went away to get the luggage and Gijs said something to Lien, who smiled and nodded and disappeared through the archway to the kitchen.

'I'll show you your room, dear girl—Lien's gone to put the supper on and Jaap will be up in a few minutes with your cases.' He took her arm and they went up the staircase together, to a passage with two doors in it, one of which he opened. He said matter-of-factly: 'The bathroom's through that door. I'm across the landing, first door on the left, if you should want anything. I'll be back in five minutes.'

He was as good as his word; they went downstairs together, to a cheerfully lighted dining-room, to eat the supper Lien had prepared for them and to drink the champagne Gijs opened, and when they had finished he said:

'You must be very tired, my dear. Go to bed and I'll tell Lien not to call you tomorrow. Ring when you wake and she will bring you your breakfast.'

It sounded super, but Serena, mindful that she was now a housewife, protested: 'I'll get up, I'd much rather. Haven't you got your surgery in the morning? What time do you leave the house? Can't I have breakfast with you?'—she hesitated—'that's if you'd like me to.'

He had his head bent as he fondled German's ears. The little dog had given them an overwhelming welcome, and now he was standing on his short back legs, his head on his master's knee. 'I should like that very much. Breakfast is at half past seven, so why not come down in your dressing gown—you can dress afterwards. I shall be home for lunch about half past twelve, unless I get held up at the hospital. What will you do?'

'Do you mind if I go round the house again? I'm sure Lien will want me to see the cupboards and things and talk about food, and I hope she'll let me do the shopping when I've learnt more about it all.'

'Of course she will, but remember that later on, when you've found your feet, you're coming to give me a helping hand sometimes.'

The little glow inside spread; it was nice to be wanted. Her mouth curved into a smile. 'I shall like that.' She got up and he got up too and came round the table to her. 'Goodnight, Gijs.' She paused, considering how she should say what she was so anxious for him to know. 'I have a lot to thank you for, and I'm very grateful. I'll try and be a good wife—the sort of wife you want, I mean.'

'You're sure you know the kind of wife I want, dear girl?' he asked the question with a little smile.

'You said—that is, I think I know. I like you very much, Gijs—I'll be loyal to you, even in my thoughts.' She flushed brightly as she spoke because it hadn't been easy to say, and perhaps he knew that because he put his hands on her shoulders and bent and kissed her cheek, a calm, reassuring kiss, not at all the kind of kiss he had given her in the car.

'I know that, Serena, and never forget that I... like you too. Friendship is a very sound basis for marriage.'

He went to the foot of the stairs with her and stood watching her until she turned the corner under the arch. She turned and smiled at him there and then went on up to the top, to cross the landing to the room which was to be hers.

She was called in the morning by Lien with a cup of tea and when she looked at her watch it was to see that it was almost half past seven. It took her only a couple of minutes to wash her face and hands, comb her hair back and run downstairs to find Gijs, with German at his heels, coming in from the street.

'I'm late,' she declared, breathless and still a little sleepy.

'No—I walked German before breakfast so that we could have more time together over breakfast. Good morning, Serena.' He came towards her and she lifted her face for his kiss, but missed the gleam in his eyes.

'I could take German in the mornings, if you like, then you would have more time.'

'So I would, but you see, German walks me too. I don't see why we shouldn't go together and have breakfast a little later, do you?'

They went into the little sitting-room where breakfast was laid and Serena sat down and poured coffee for them both. 'I'd like that,' she said. 'Are you going to be busy today?'

She listened while he told her, and although she

hadn't missed hospital since she had left Queen's, she found her interest quickening as he described some of his cases.

'Do you do any surgery?'

'Only in an emergency. I prefer general practice and paediatrics.'

'You don't look after the whole island?'

'Good lord, no, but the patients are scattered round it. You've been across the island, you've seen how isolated some of the farms are.'

He swallowed coffee and got to his feet. 'You shall come with me sometimes if you've nothing better to do, it will be a splendid way of getting to know the island. I must go.' He kissed her cheek and she felt the pressure of his hand on her shoulder and heard the door close quietly behind him.

She wandered upstairs presently and bathed and dressed, telephoned her mother because Gijs had reminded her to do so and then went downstairs to find Lien. It was easier going around the house than she had expected; Lien might not understand English, but she was sharp enough, and opening and shutting cupboards and drawers and pointing out their contents was just as effective as talking about them. Pleased with themselves and each other, they retired to the kitchen and with the aid of a dictionary, settled on the menus for lunch and dinner. It was almost eleven o'clock by then and Lien said firmly: '*Koffie, Jonkvrouw,*' and Serena, a little startled at being addressed so, went into the garden and drank the delicious brew Lien brought out to her, and because it was high summer and a lovely day and the garden was green and peaceful and she felt suddenly peaceful inside too, she went to sleep.

She awoke to find German's inquisitive, slightly

anxious eyes within inches of her own and the sun blotted out by Gijs's shadow. She sat up at once, feeling foolish, exclaiming: 'I fell asleep, I never meant to—have you been waiting for me to wake up?'

'My dear girl, you were tired out—a long journey after the wedding and everything strange. How did the housekeeping go?' He grinned at her and she found herself smiling back at him, feeling light-hearted.

'Splendidly. Lien's such a dear. What a treasure she is!'

'Yes. I take care to surround myself with trea-sures. Come inside, I've something to show you before lunch.'

They went into the sitting-room in the old part of the house, its doors invitingly open on to the garden. Someone had filled it with flowers, and it smelled sweet, the sweetness tempered by the faint smell of beeswax. There was a hamper on one of the side tables. Gijs opened it and lifted out a very small Basset hound. 'For you,' he said.

Serena took the small creature in her arms and stroked its ears. She stared at Gijs, wanting, for some reason which she couldn't fathom, to burst into tears, perhaps because he had remembered her once saying she would like one, and had wanted to give her pleasure. She tucked the puppy firmly into the crook of her arm and put a hand on Gijs's arm. 'Thank you,' she spoke with fervour. 'How kind you are! I shall love him very much.' She kissed the puppy's nose. 'Will German like him?'

'I imagine so—they travelled together in the car for a good deal of the morning. What will you call him?'

'Oh, something short and easy, so that Lien and Jaap can say his name easily.' She closed her eyes the better to think. 'Gus,' she essayed, 'do you like that for a name?'

'Yes, it suits him, but you'd better try it on him first.'

The puppy approved, if by being licked by a small pink tongue was anything to go by. They went to the dining-room, German walking importantly in front of them, Gus still firmly in Serena's arms, and once they were there the problem of what to do with him during the meal was solved by German, who got into his basket as he always did and obligingly moved over to make room for Gus beside him.

The meal was a pleasant one, for there was Gijs's work to talk about, and when they were finished and were in the sitting-room drinking their coffee he asked her if she would like the idea of going on his afternoon rounds with him.

Serena looked up from the absorbing task of offering Gus milk in a saucer.

'Oh, may I? I should like that very much. When do you want to go?'

'In ten minutes or so—if I'm not held up too long we'll be able to get back in time for tea. I've a surgery this evening at half past five.'

'I suppose you wouldn't want me to come to the surgery too?' She was unconscious of the wistfulness of her voice.

'There's nothing I should like better. Father's still in England, as you know, and so is Laurens, and I'm single-handed. Rene's a great help, but we could use another pair of hands.'

She went to get ready for the afternoon's round then, feeling happy because she was going to be useful, even in a small way, and Gijs had sounded pleased because she had asked, and she wanted to please him.

There were quite a number of patients to visit—Gijs chose to do the country patients first—Dreischor, and then a farm on a lonely road in the centre of the island and then on to Brouwershaven, where he disappeared into a very small house in a narrow street which barely permitted the car's width. From there they went along the narrow brick roads with flat fields on either side, to Elkerzee, a very small village indeed, where, Gijs told her, there was an outbreak of measles amongst the children. He visited several houses and when he came back to the car, said: 'Well, one more, and then back to Zierikzee.'

It was almost five o'clock when at length Gijs stopped outside his own front door. There was another car parked there, a Mini—of a pleasing blue and very new. Gijs had a parked behind it and when they got out took some keys from his pocket and put them in Serena's hand.

'Yours,' he said almost laconically. 'We'll go for a run this evening to make sure that you remember which side of the road to drive on.'

She gaped at him, clutching the keys. 'Mine? For me?'

He gave her a lazy smile. 'Why, yes, my dear. You may want to go shopping or visiting and certainly to see Mother and I shan't always be free to drive you. You'll need your own car.'

She was peering inside it. It was upholstered in dove grey and her name and address were engraved on a small oval disc on the dashboard. She said softly: 'Oh, Gijs—thank you! I can never thank you enough. I don't know what to say.'

He had opened the house door and she went past him into the cool hall.

'I'm glad you like it.' His placid face looked mildly pleased, no more. 'I expect tea will be in the sitting-room—shall we go through?'

She put Gus down and the little dog trotted off in German's wake. Gijs flung an arm round her shoulders as they went through the house and remarked: 'I should think we might leave Gus at home while we're in the surgery, don't you? He can have a nap in the kitchen, German will keep him company.'

The surgery, when they reached it half an hour later, was stuffed with people. It was in a cul-de-sac leading off Paternosterstraat, a flat-faced house the whole of whose ground floor was taken up by two consulting-rooms, a waiting-room and a little room squeezed in by the front door, where the patients gave their names and the notes were kept. Upstairs, Serena had time to notice, there were curtains at the windows and she wondered who lived there. She would ask Gijs, but not now, because it was already half past five and there were more than enough patients for him to see.

There was a young woman in the cubbyhole and Gijs greeted her cheerfully as they went in and said: 'Serena, this is Rene, she's leaving to get married at the end of the week. There's another girl coming soon, but in the meantime I'd be eternally grateful if you would give a hand—we've no nurse this evening either.'

Serena beamed at him, glad of an opportunity to help. She shook Rene's hand and squeezed herself into the cubby-hole, wondering how she could possibly be of use, for her Dutch, to say the least, was only fragmental. But Rene, she discovered after a few minutes, understood basic English at least and spoke a little too. Serena discovered too that it was a question of getting the patients' names right, for the filing system was exactly the same as it was in England and as far as she could see, the surgery was run on exactly the same lines as an English GP's. Under Rene's excellent tuition she began to make a little headway even though many of the names were quite unpronounceable, but there were easy ones and she was quick to learn and had a good memory. She began to enjoy herself.

The last patient went soon after half past six in an evening which was still very warm. Serena went out to the car with Gijs, shook hands with Rene who lived just down the street, and got in beside him. 'Nice work,' he praised her lightly as he edged the car back into Paternosterstraat. 'Do you think you could manage for a few days on your own until the new girl comes?'

Serena glowed. 'Oh, yes. I enjoyed it, though some of the names are very difficult.'

'Just at first,' he assured her comfortably. 'I don't know how you feel about it, but the headmaster of the MAVO school here is a splendid teacher and a brilliant scholar. I wondered if you would like him to give you lessons in Dutch.'

'It's funny you should say that, for I had only made up my mind half an hour ago that I would find someone to teach me—I was going to surprise you.'

She missed the sudden gleam in his eyes. 'How delightful. I promise not to ask how you're getting on and then you can still surprise me.'

They were back outside the house once more.

'Would you still like to try the Mini?'

'Please.' She was as excited as a small girl with a new doll; she could hardly wait for him to cram himself into the seat beside her before switching on the engine.

She acquitted herself very well. 'But keep to the island for a little while,' Gijs advised her, 'and make sure you know all the signs—you'll have to take a test, you know. I'll arrange that as soon as I can.'

She nodded happily. 'Where shall I put her? I don't even know if you've got a garage.'

'Lord yes, I'll show you where it is.'

It was in fact down a narrow *steeg* behind the house, built against the back wall of the garden and next to the cottage. Serena hadn't noticed the door in the wall by Lien's little home; it led into the back of a roomy garage which, a long time ago, must have been a house. Its exterior had been faithfully restored, even the garage doors were of massive oak with iron bolts and hinges. It was easy enough to reach by running the car up the narrow street beside the house and then turning sharply into the *steeg*. Serena, determined to deserve her present, drove the Mini round and parked it beside the Bentley.

'There's a key to the garage on that bunch,' Gijs explained as they went back through the garden door, 'and if you should happen to lose it Jaap has duplicates of every key I possess.' He sauntered across the grass, an arm on her shoulder. 'What time is dinner?' he wanted to know.

'The same time as always,' said Serena. 'Lien told me the times you liked your meals, and I'm not going to change anything for you.'

His arm felt a little heavier. 'No? We shall see!'

His voice had sounded strange and she didn't

know how to answer him, instead she said: 'I think I'll go up and change my dress—it's been a lovely day.' She smiled at him and suffered faint chagrin when he agreed with a casual good humour that evinced no real interest.

The week went in a flash; she wondered at the end of each full day how she could have imagined that she would never have enough to do. And in two days' time, when her parents-in-law returned from England, Gijs had assured her that his mother would take her visiting each day to meet their friends. 'And we shall have to give a dinner party later on,' he warned her, 'but first we shall get a great number of invitations. Mother will give a reception for us very shortly so that all the people who would have come to our wedding if we had been married here can come and wish us well and take a look at the bride.'

'Oh,' uttered Serena, 'I shall be terrified!'

'No, you won't. We just stand together and shake hands with everyone and I'll tell you what to say. I daresay we shall dance afterwards.'

He dismissed the whole thing carelessly, but Serena became thoughtful so that presently he said: 'Something worrying you, dear girl?'

'Clothes—what do I wear?'

'It will be black ties. Something pretty and bride-like. Couldn't you wear your wedding dress?'

Serena eyed him with kindly pity. How like a man! What woman would want to appear at her first important evening function wearing her wedding gown, just as though she hadn't got anything else? 'Not really,' she told him. 'You see, it's got a little train and it looks like a wedding dress.'

His eyes twinkled. 'How stupid of me! Shall we

go and buy something? I could manage Saturday afternoon—we could try Amsterdam, or failing that, den Haag.'

She shook her head. 'No, I don't think there's any need. I've a rather pretty dress which I think might do. Long, you know—cream gauze over silk with a pink velvet sash. I bought it because it was so beautiful. . .'

'What a good reason, it sounds just right. And that reminds me to tell you that I have opened an account for you at my bank—across the canal, next to the hotel.' He had given her a cheque book then and mentioned the sum he had paid in for her. 'Quarterly,' he added casually, and ignored her protest, 'and I don't expect you to pay for the Mini out of it—have anything you need for it put on my account.'

'But you're too generous. How can I possibly spend all that money?' she remonstrated, but all he did was laugh. 'Have a good try,' was all he said, and: 'Remember I told you not to let it become important, Serena.'

They went to dinner with Gijs's parents on the evening of their return, and Serena, who had been feeling a little nervous about it, was overwhelmed by their greeting. They sat round the dinner table, making a leisurely meal while they gave her messages from her family and then went on to tell her how lovely the wedding had been, and her mother-in-law interrupted herself to send her husband upstairs to fetch the wedding photos which Serena's mother had entrusted to her care. 'And now we must introduce you to everyone,' she went on enthusiastically. 'I shall, of course, give a reception for you both—we had better have a room at the Mondragon, and you must come with me when I go visiting, my dear, if you can bear with an old woman's company, and in that way you will get to know everyone very quickly. Has Gijs taken you anywhere?'

'He's had no time,' Serena smiled across the table at him. 'There's been the surgery to run single-handed, you know. I've been going down each evening and helping.'

Her mother-in-law gave a faint shriek. 'Gijs,' she demanded, 'how could you ask of Serena that she should work, and she a bride of only a few days.'

'But he didn't ask—' began Serena, but was interrupted gently by her husband.

'Dear Mama, did we never tell you that one of the conditions of our marriage was that Serena should help me from time to time?' He spoke seriously, but his eyes danced with laughter and when he and Serena exchanged glances his mother declared: 'I don't believe a word of it—you make the joke. There is no need for Serena to work, there is enough for her to do with that house to manage and presently the children.'

At which remark Serena blushed, a slow, painful pinkening which spread over her lovely face until she felt as though she was on fire and which was fanned to an even more maddening brilliance by Gijs's bland: 'Just so, Mama,' and his wicked look directed at herself. She sat, fuming silently that she was fool enough to blush in such a gauche and stupid fashion, and thanked heaven silently when Gijs drew the conversation on to himself, giving her time to regain her normal complexion. Presently her father-in-law went to fetch some wedding presents they had offered to bring with them, and these kept everyone agreeably occupied until she and Gijs left, half an hour later. She talked about them, at length and quite unnecessarily, for the entire journey home.

She began her Dutch lessons the following day. It had been arranged that she would have them each afternoon from half past four until just after five, which allowed her to give Gijs tea at four o'clock if he were home, and left her free for the surgery in the evenings. The new girl was there now, but the secretary never came in the evening, and the nurse was on holiday. The new girl was nice but a little slow, and although now that he was back, Gijs's father came in to help, Laurens hadn't returned yet. Serena would have liked to ask why, but Gijs had told her nothing and he might find it rather strange of her to inquire—as if she were still interested in Laurens.

By some magic on the part of Jonkvrouw van Amstel, the reception she had declared obligatory to give on their behalf had been arranged for the Saturday evening after her return. How she had managed to do this in such a short space of time was something Serena couldn't guess at. Presumably she had spent a day at the telephone, inviting everyone on the formidable list she had shown Serena. And Serena, not to be outdone by her mother-in-law's organizing powers, invited her and her father-in-law to dinner on the evening of the reception, for it would be the easiest thing in the world to go the few hundred yards to the restaurant in time to receive the guests, and besides, she had a nagging, unspoken wish to show them how well she had settled down as a good wife to Gijs.

She spent a great deal of time and thought over the dinner, and what with her natural anxiety to prove herself a good hostess and an equally natural desire to shine at the evening's entertainment, she was a bundle of nerves by the time the evening arrived. Indeed, her temper, already frayed round the edges, was quite uncertain by the time Gijs—unaccountably late—got home. He found her wandering around the dining-room table, clad in her dressing gown, her hair in an untidy plait, frowning at its exquisite silver and china, and when he inquired cheerfully if she shouldn't leave everything to Jaap, she said snappishly that she certainly would and what did it matter anyway, they might just as well have something out of a tin. She then burst into tears and made for the stairs where he overtook her easily enough and catching her by the shoulders, turned her round to face him. 'What's gone wrong, my pretty?' he wanted to know.

Serena sniffed, feeling slightly better already because he had called her his pretty.

'Nothing,' she managed, and sniffed again, and then as Gijs still waited, wisely aware that the nothing was a mere figure of speech, she went on. 'At least nothing much. I—I made a Charlotte Russe and it b-broke when I turned it out. Lien put it together again, but. . .and Gus made a puddle on the sitting-room carpet, and I know my hair's going to look awful!'

She ended on a faint wail and peered up at his kind face.

The hands on her shoulders gathered her close as he kissed her reassuringly.

'My poor little wife—but none of these things seem fatal to our evening. I presume Gus's accident has been dealt with, and no one need know about the Charlotte Russe. I shan't tell and I'm sure Lien won't—as for your hair, I find it very pretty as it is.'

Which remark she found so amusing that she giggled and Gijs said bracingly: 'That's better. Come along and have a drink, we've plenty of time. Are my things put out, by the way?'

She nodded, looking quite beautiful despite her red eyes and tangled hair. 'Yes—I did them after tea. I hope they're what you want.'

'Bound to be,' he sounded comfortably certain about it. 'What are we doing to eat, or is it a secret?'

She told him. 'Well, Gurkas Norge for starters—you know, the Galloping Gourmet. . .'

'I don't know, but I daresay I'll catch up with you as you go along—a recipe book, perhaps?' he hazarded.

'A man—a cook. Cucumber and anchovies and cream cheese and sour cream and some caviare—they're rather expensive, I'm afraid.'

'But absolutely necessary for our first dinner party. What's next?'

She giggled and then said solemnly. 'Potts' Point Fish Pot,' and joined in his bellow of laughter. 'It's flounders and lobster and mushrooms and white wine—oh, and brandy. . .'

'Dear girl, you've excelled yourself. Don't tell me any more or I shall feel compelled to go to the kitchen and eat the lot. Quite obviously it will be the inspiration of the evening.'

'You think so?' They started to walk towards the sittingroom. 'There's the Charlotte Russe for afters, and coffee, of course. Only I don't know about the drinks.'

'I'll see to those,' he gave her a Dubonnet. 'Drink this up and then go and put on your party dress.'

A few minutes later she was on her way upstairs,

to be arrested half way by his quiet voice, reminding her:

'Remember what I told you, Serena? You're going to meet Laurens, but as my wife. I know you saw him at our wedding, but weddings aren't quite real, are they, and this is.'

She looked down at him standing below her, his hands in his pockets, half smiling, quite unworried. She could think of nothing to say in answer; she nodded briefly and went on up to her room. It was while she was dressing that she realized why he had said it; he was afraid that meeting Laurens again would be unbearably painful for her, that she would need all her pride and courage to speak to him. It was strange that now she probed her feelings further, she didn't think she was going to feel any of these things. Laurens, in some mysterious way, had faded. She stared at her reflection and wondered why. She might have gone on wondering for quite some time if Gijs hadn't knocked on the door and come in. He was quite ready and wore the air of a man who had spent at least an hour and that a leisurely one, in dressing himself. She wondered how he did it and wondered too how she had ever thought him slow-moving, as obedient to his request she stood up for his inspection.

The dress had been a happy choice, she knew; its deep clotted cream showed up her tan and made her dark hair even darker and her eyes more brilliant. She had put on the pearls and had been fiddling with some earrings; now she laid them down on the dressing-table, spread her skirts and asked childishly, 'Will I do?'

He came and stood close to her, looking not at her dress, but at her face.

'Oh, you'll do, my dear. You've never looked lovelier, excepting on our wedding day.' He put a hand in his pocket and took out something. 'You told me your sash was pink. I hope these will match well enough.'

A pair of earrings lay in his palm, bright ruby stars outlined with diamonds and with a single pearl drop. Serena stared at them for a long minute before she looked at him. 'For me?' She repeated his words and touched them gently. 'But they're magnificent!'

'Great-grandmother's this time, and this goes with them.' He added a bracelet to the earrings; it lay there, winking and twinkling in the light, a lovely ornate band of rubies and diamonds and pearls, held together by gold links.

Serena goggled a little. 'Gijs, I—they're so lovely. Do you really want me to have them?'

'Indeed, yes. And there's this besides.' A brooch this time, of the same splendour as the bracelet, its pearl drops hanging down in a milky fringe.

She said, breathless: 'I'll put them on,' and hooked the earrings into her ears and held out an arm so that he might fasten the bracelet and then asked. 'The brooch—shall I wear it in the centre or a little to one side?'

He gave her a considered look. 'The centre, I think. They become you very well, Serena.'

She fastened the brooch carefully and turned to inspect her person in the mirror. The jewels were most becoming to her, as was the dress. She smiled at his reflected face and turned to kiss him. 'Thank you, Gijs. You give me so much, and I do so little.'

He said a little harshly: 'But I ask for nothing, Serena,' and then seeing her eyes widen went on in his usual mild voice: 'I see the hair went up without any difficulties after all. Shall we go down? Father and Mother should be here very soon.'

Much later that night, lying in her great bed, Serena looked back over the evening and knew it to have been a success, and fun too. Dinner had been all it should be and had been eaten with gratifying appetite by her guests, Gus had behaved with circumspection and she had sat at table, happily aware that she looked her best, that her mother and father-in-law liked her and that Gijs was proud of her. She had arrived at the hotel, knowing that these factors had given her poise and confidence; when she paused at the entrance to the room where the reception was to be held and caught Gijs's eyes, no longer half hidden beneath sleepy lids, but gleaming with admiration, she had coloured faintly under his stare and smiled a little, and he had crossed to her side and taken her arm and murmured: 'Enchanting Serena,' and smiled with such warmth that she felt emboldened to say: 'Oh, Gijs, it's all right, isn't it? Us—our marriage—is it how you wanted it?'

She gave him an anxious, intent look, dimly conscious that if he was content, she was not. And she should have been; she had a good-looking husband who was goodness itself and kind too, and they were great friends, which was more than one could say of some husbands and wives. She had a lovely home too and more money than she knew what to do with—and Gus, and the rubies. . .

His voice had reassured her: 'Dear girl, you are exactly what I wanted. Now come over here and stand with Mother and Father—that's right, between Father and me. You don't need to speak unless you're spoken to in English, just smile.'

So she had smiled and shaken hands and allowed

herself to be stared at, albeit in the kindest possible manner, and forgotten almost all the names Gijs was at pains to tell her; she had never seen so many strange faces, which made Laurens's familiar good looks all the more of a shock when he appeared suddenly before her. She met his blue intent gaze with dignity and a smile which, try as she would, trembled a little at the edges, because she had been dreading this meeting and now it was upon her.

She tried now to remember what she had said; something light and casual while the memory of Gijs's words that evening lifted her chin a fraction of an inch higher and steadied her smile. Gijs had helped too, as she had known he would, slipping an arm into hers and talking easily to his cousin, asking about his leg and his probable return to the practice, drawing her into the conversation without any apparent effort. Laurens moved away presently and Gijs said pleasantly, in a voice loud enough for those around to hear: 'How well Laurens looks, darling.'

He had never called her darling before, she reminded herself, lying wide awake in the lovely room; she would think about that presently. At the time she had no chance to do more than feel surprised; she was far too taken up with the necessity of telling Gijs something. She managed to whisper: 'I didn't really see him, Gijs—it didn't matter—it wasn't the same.'

It was three days later when Gijs asked her if she would go to the surgery with him that evening because Ina, the new receptionist, had tonsillitis and couldn't work.

She walked to the surgery because Gijs had rung her up during the afternoon and told her that he couldn't get home for tea and would she meet him there. The little town was quiet, the shops were closed for the day and almost everyone, even the tourists, was indoors getting ready for their evening meal. The weather was quiet too—the unnatural quiet of a pending storm. Serena, who hated thunder, looked at the sky and was glad to see that the clouds were still only a vague menace on the horizon.

The surgery was already full although there was quite ten minutes before it would open. She dived into the little room by the door and began the laborious job getting out the patients' notes.

Gijs arrived five minutes later, unhurried and quiet, but when he paused briefly to speak to her, she saw that he was tired. He had told her that Laurens would be coming and, she thought, a good thing too, for Gijs was doing too much. Laurens turned up twenty minutes later. She saw, with faint amusement, his look of amazement at seeing her there; the look was swept away, replaced by the gay smile she had found so irresistible and which now, surprisingly, left her unmoved.

'Hullo,' he said lightly, 'earning your keep already? Don't tell me old Gijs has sacked the new girl and given you the job of unpaid assistant?'

He had sounded spiteful and she didn't allow him to finish. She didn't raise her voice, but it held her contempt, as did her pretty face, scarlet with the strength of her feelings.

'How dare you speak of Gijs like that!—He's worth a hundred of you, he works twice as hard and he's the most generous man alive. . .' She paused for breath, as astonished as he was at her outburst.

'Well, well, what a nasty temper! I never knew before that you couldn't stand a tease.' He turned on his heel and she said quietly: 'You weren't teasing, Laurens.'

She was kept busy after that—too busy, so that she muddled up the cards of the two Mevrouw Anne Smits who had, by a strange coincidence, presented themselves at the same surgery at the same time, and sent them to the wrong doctor.

Laurens's door opened first to disgorge the wrong Mevrouw Smit, and following hard on her heels, Laurens. 'Good God, Serena,' he began impatiently, 'surely you can do something as simple as sending me my own patients?'

Serena, struggling to find a missing card, looked up briefly, determined not to lose her cool but a little pink all the same.

'I'm sorry. There are two Anne Smits here and I've got them muddled. You had the wrong one.'

'Of course I got the wrong one. Send in my patient and for heaven's sake don't keep me hanging about.'

'I don't really think you mean to speak to my wife in that fashion, do you, Laurens?' Gijs's voice was almost a drawl and he was smiling faintly, but something in his look caused his cousin to say hastily: '*Hemel*, no—sorry, Serena.' He smiled at her briefly and went back into his surgery, sweeping the right Mrs Smit with him.

Gijs said nothing more, only asked her about some tests she had managed to fit in somehow or other, and presently went back to his own consulting-room and closed the door.

The two men finished more or less together, but Serena, bogged down in strange outlandish names, was still opening and shutting drawers, tidying things away and filing letters for future reference. The telephone rang again and she put out a hand to take the receiver, but Gijs took it from her. 'You've enough to do, dear girl.' He eyed the neat lists of names and addresses she had compiled from the calls which had come in during surgery hours. 'I'll take it.'

He had dealt with it when Laurens came out of his room, his bag in his hand. 'I'm off,' he told them. 'I've a date and a couple of visits to do first.' He waved airily and Serena, finished at last, shutting doors and fastening windows, heard the Jag roar down the narrow street. She looked at Gijs. 'Have you any calls?' she asked.

'Yes, I must go to the hospital and see how that man I sent in this morning is doing, and I've a couple of patients to see in the centre of the island—shall I drop you off first?'

'May I come with you? Gus and German will be OK, I took them for a walk after my lesson.'

For answer he opened the door of the car, shut it after her and got in himself. 'Nice,' he remarked. 'The day has seemed very long; lunch was a rush, wasn't it, and I missed tea at home.'

'Would you like to stop now and I'll get you some. It won't take a minute.'

His hand brushed her knee lightly. 'My thoughtful wife—but I'd better get on, I think. There's a baby case due and I like to be free for those.'

'Yes, of course. Is the hospital going to take long?'

He shook his head. 'Ten minutes. Would you like to come in?'

She would have loved that—to see where he worked and meet the people he worked with, but it might delay him.

They were still out in the flat countryside, with Zierikzee visible on the horizon, when the thunder clouds suddenly bundled together to assume an awe-inspiring blackness. The wind came first, tearing at the Bentley, then the rain and lastly lightning, cracking through the sky in what must have been a magnificent sight to anyone who liked such spectacles of Nature. Serena sat rigid, trying not to hear the thunder bellowing around them; searching frantically for a spot in the wide sky which the lightning hadn't yet found. In the end she closed her eyes, but opened them instantly when Gijs said: 'Come closer. I didn't know you disliked storms—they're rather extravagant here at times. We're nearly home.'

She crept near to him. He felt solid and safe and he hadn't laughed at her for being afraid.

They played backgammon after dinner and she wondered if it was to keep her occupied because of the storm still raging outside. But presently it rolled away and Serena said goodnight and went upstairs, yawning realistically but longing to stay with him until the last rumble had faded and the last faint lightning had flickered itself out. But she knew Gijs had his letters to read as well as the pile of medical journals which arrived each week. She got ready for bed rapidly and got into bed. If the storm got worse she could always go downstairs and sit with him.

She wakened to lightning flickering round the room and the distant rumble of thunder once more, and because it was too hot to pull the sheet over her head she switched on the bedside lights, which, while not attempting to compete with the electricity outside, afforded some measure of comfort. She had been uneasily awake for ten minutes or more when she became aware of vague noises downstairs, and very faintly, Gus barking. It was half past two, Gijs would have been in bed hours ago and if he was going out on a case the dogs, used to his footfall in the house, wouldn't have barked. Lien and Jaap were in their own little cottage—the obvious answer was that someone was downstairs—someone who shouldn't be there. She lay worrying about it for a moment or two and when she could bear it no longer, got out of bed, put on her dressing gown, thrust her feet into slippers and opened the door.

The hall was quiet and dim and smelled faintly of flowers which she had arranged earlier in the day. She went through the arch towards the kitchen, going quickly before she had time to be afraid and as she drew level with the study door, it opened and Gijs came out, his bag in his hand.

Serena stood still, her hand over her mouth like a frightened little girl and said in a voice squeaky with fright: 'Oh, you're going out on a case.'

'Yes, darling. Did I disturb you? Gus mistook me for an intruder, I think. I'm sorry. It's the baby— remember the second farm we went to this afternoon.' He passed her on the way to the door and then came back, kissed her on the mouth and went outside into the storm without a backward glance.

Serena stood where he had left her, staring at the shut door, wishing she was with him, storm or no storm. Presently she saw the lights from the car sweep past the house and when they had quite disappeared, she went to the kitchen, made some tea and sat down to drink it with Gus in her lap and German snoring companionably in his basket. It was pleasant there, the curtains had been drawn against the night, so that the lightning seemed less frightening, the scrubbed table smelt nicely of soap and the light over the sink shone cheerfully on the rows of pans which were Lien's pride. The storm grumbled its way round the sky and Gus, warm and secure, went to sleep, his head, swathed in its ridiculous ears, pushed under her arm. In a little while she went to sleep herself.

Gijs was in the room when she woke up, and the beginnings of a pale dawn were edging round the curtains. She jumped up, dislodging an indignant Gus. Serena hadn't meant to go to sleep. She tossed her hair out of her eyes, fighting a desire to close them again.

'I'll make you some tea—it must be morning. Was everything all right?'

She studied his face as she put on the kettle. He was tired, more than tired, bone weary, but he smiled at her with his usual good humour.

'Now this is what I call luxury—a wife waiting for me with tea! Yes, everything was fine—just the baby held us up for a bit—a breech.'

'A boy?'

'Yes—they're delighted; the other two are girls.' He put his case down on the table and sat himself down beside it. 'Have you been here all night?'

'Yes—after you had gone I came to see if Gus was all right, and it was so cosy. I made some tea and then Gus got on my lap—he and German were good company.'

She made the tea and fetched two mugs from the dresser. 'My poor girl,' he said, 'you've had a bad night, but the storm's over now. It will be a lovely day.'

She looked at the clock on the wall; it was almost five. 'Did you get to bed at all before you were called out?' she wanted to know.

'Yes—for a couple of hours.' He smiled a little.

'Don't worry about me, Serena, this happens quite frequently, you know.'

'Yes. Will you go to bed now? There are still two hours. . .'

He finished his tea and got up from the table. 'A good idea—and you?'

She was suddenly shy. 'I'll just clear up these things.' For something to do she went to the window and drew the curtains aside, letting in the morning light. It fell upon Gijs's face, highlighting its lines and furrows and bristly chin. She stared at him as though she had never seen him before, knowing in that moment that it was the face of the man she loved. She might have gone on staring for ever if he hadn't asked: 'What's the matter? Why do you stare so?'

'You're tired out,' she managed in a matter-of-fact voice. 'Do go to bed.' She thought he hadn't heard her, for he didn't answer, but after a moment or two he went to the door, and with his hand on the handle asked her: 'Do you know how beautiful you are, Serena?'

He didn't wait for her to answer. She heard him going quietly up to his room and when the door shut gently, she took the mugs to the sink and started to wash them up. She did it very slowly, while her tired mind absorbed the fact that she had fallen in love with her husband, who, when they had agreed to marry, had made it abundantly plain, in the nicest possible way, that his feelings for her were no more than affectionate.

CHAPTER EIGHT

OF course she didn't sleep. She went upstairs, hardly knowing that she was crying, and lay down on the bed, thinking back to the day at Queen's when she had first met Gijs. He had never been anything but kind, she told herself tearfully, and she had been ungrateful and thoughtless of his feelings. In the darkness she squirmed at the memory of her cool reception of him when he had arrived at her home to drive her back to hospital; she had thought then how marvellous Laurens had been to think of her, while in actual fact it had cost him no effort at all, only to persuade his cousin to drive miles to collect a girl he had barely met. She wondered briefly why Gijs had done it. The doubt, still faint, crept into her head that perhaps he hadn't married her for the reasons he had given her—they had seemed so sensible and reasonable at the time—but out of pity; he liked her, she knew that, and they were friends; one did a lot for a friend in trouble, and she had been alone and very unhappy.

She rolled over and thumped the pillows, wondering miserably what she should do. It would be embarrassing for him if she were to tell him, without any warning, that she had discovered that she loved him, but if she didn't, he would never know, would he? Perhaps it would be better if he didn't.

She got up and started walking up and down and round and round, and her brain, soggy with her crying, refused to think calmly or sensibly any more.

184

She went and had a bath and when she got back into the bedroom it was to find her early morning tea waiting for her. She drank it thankfully and set about the task of disguising her tear-stained face. She must have succeeded very well because when she went down to breakfast a little later, Gijs accorded her the briefest of glances and went back to his post, and presently got up to go. 'A heavy day,' he excused himself. 'Don't expect me home for lunch, Serena—I'll telephone if I find I can't get back for dinner, so don't wait for me if I'm late.'

Serena met his eyes briefly. 'You don't want me at the surgery this evening?'

He shook his head. 'Ina will be back, I think. Have a nice day.'

He went away without kissing her.

She spent that day, and the succeeding days, doing a variety of things to make herself believe that she was neither lonely nor unhappy. Gijs seemed to be busy; beyond their brief walk and the briefer breakfast following it and a rather silent meal at night, she saw little of him, and when they were together she sensed a reserve that she had never noticed before, a reserve which she didn't attempt to break down for fear of showing her own feelings.

It was two weeks after the storm, on a dull, rainy afternoon, while Lien and Jaap were in their cottage and she had the house to herself, that someone knocked thunderously on the street door. Serena hurried to answer it; Gijs hadn't been home for lunch, perhaps it was someone with an urgent message for him. The girl at the door was quite young, in her teens, and quite distraught, so that she was prevented from speaking with any degree of coherence. Serena waited patiently for her to calm down a little, and then, in her newly acquired Dutch, asked what was the matter. The girl began again, this time more slowly and certainly more clearly. She had slipped out, she explained—adding a little wildly that it had only been for a moment, leaving the two children she looked after while their mother was at work; little children, Serena gathered. They had been playing together in the kitchen—the girl shrugged, an old room with a rotten floor—and they had been jumping up and down as children will, and while they had been alone there had been an accident. It was vital that the doctor came at once.

'He's not here,' said Serena, struggling with her verbs. 'Can't you telephone the hospital?' She saw that the girl didn't understand her very well and repeated 'Telephone?' and was met with such a look of fear that she drew back in astonishment.

'Not my children,' said the girl at last. So that was it! She had been trusted to mind the children and she had broken her trust and didn't want the mother to find out. She would have to be persuaded—but in the meantime the children might be in real need. Serena pointed to herself and said '*Verpleegster*,' a rather comical-sounding word, she considered, but it did mean 'Nurse' in Dutch and at least the girl understood what she had said, because relief spread over her young, frightened face. Perhaps the accident wasn't too bad if she thought a nurse would do. Serena decided to go with her and have a look, it would be quicker in the long run than standing there arguing, and perhaps by then the girl would have calmed down and fetch a doctor if he was wanted. She could ring Gijs herself, of course, but he had said that he was going to be busy and now he would be out on his afternoon rounds, anyway, it might not be necessary to have a doctor at all. She ushered the girl out into the street and closed the door behind them.

They crossed to the other side of the canal and walked rapidly and silently past the Melkmarkt, then plunged down a narrow alley which led them into a cobbled street which Serena recognized at once because it had the peculiar name of Hem. Half-way down its length the girl turned into another narrow alley, lined with old and rather decrepit houses. Into one of these she hurried, muttering to herself, Serena hard at her heels. But despite her hurry, the girl stopped to shut the door carefully behind her before leading the way down a minuscule hallway to the kitchen at its end. She had been right, the floor was rotten; it had given way in one corner, the snapped-off boards standing up in splinters. There was something else in the corner too, a small arm trailing on the ground. Serena dropped on her knees and felt the boards creak under her. The owner of the arm was lying below her on the damp stickiness of the rubble and stones beneath the floorboards, very still and quiet, and equally still, another child, a mere toddler, lay close by. The toddler lay pinned by a board across its chest, the other child, a little boy of five or thereabouts, had a great bruise over his closed eyes and a splinter of wood protruding through the shoulder of his jacket.

Serena leaned down and gently felt the smallest child's wrist. The pulse was beating quite strongly and she heaved a sigh of relief. The board across its chest didn't look heavy, so she tugged at it gently and felt a little sick when she saw that one of the nails sticking out of the board had penetrated the small chest. She would have to draw it out—but what to use for a dressing? The house hardly seemed the sort of place where she might find a first aid box set tidily on a kitchen shelf. She turned her attention to the little boy and her sickness returned, for he must have fallen on a jagged splinter of wood, for a broken sliver of it had pierced his shoulder from the back; several inches showed when she gently pulled his jacket back to have a look. She needed help, and quickly.

'Politie,' she said firmly to the girl hovering behind her, who instantly burst into tears, looking so terrified that Serena might have felt pity for her if she hadn't felt a little frightened herself.

'All right,' she said loudly and in English, 'If you won't go, I will.' The police station was in Meelstraat which was fairly close by; she could run hard all the way. She started to get up, but the girl ran to the door, banging it behind her before Serena could draw breath. Serena, creeping back into the narrow dark space under the floorboards, hoped very much that the girl had understood her and gone for help. There was nothing to do but wait and see, and meanwhile she would have to do what she could. It was awkward working in such confined space; she gritted her teeth and prised the plank off the toddler's chest; the nail had made only the smallest of puncture wounds, but she was only too well aware of the dangers of small penetrating wounds inflicted by small dirty nails. But at least, when help did arrive, the child could go immediately to hospital.

The boy was a more difficult matter; it would need two people, one to support the child and take the strain while the other drew out the splinter. She shuddered as she examined the discoloured shoulder—she didn't think that the bone was broken, but there would be extensive damage to the tissues and quite a lot of bleeding. She took their pulses, both, thank goodness, quite strong, and prayed a wordless little prayer that Gijs would come.

He did, within minutes. She heard the street door open and recognized his quiet tread and called in a steady voice, for it would never do to burst into tears and make him ashamed of her, 'Over here, Gijs, and do be careful, the floor's rotten,' and then, because she couldn't help herself, 'How did you know? I believe the girl went for the police.'

'She saw me driving down Hem and stopped me. I've sent her for more help. Make yourself small, my dear, I'm coming down too.'

His voice had sounded different—angry? She wasn't sure; a tiny piece of her mind registered the fact even while she was telling him quickly and clearly what she knew. 'I took the plank off the baby's chest,' she told him, 'you can see the puncture wound from the nail. She's got a fierce bump at the back of her head, too.' She sighed. 'They've both been unconscious all the time, thank heaven.'

He was crowded in beside her, feeling the little body carefully. 'The nail penetrated between the first and second rib,' he told her calmly, 'and there's a fractured clavicle—I can't find anything else at the moment, excepting for the bump on her head.'

He leaned across her and transferred his attention to the boy and in a minute said: 'Serena, I'm going to get behind him. When I say so, lift him up. We've got to get this damned great splinter out of him.' He glanced at her in the half dark. 'Close your eyes while I'm doing it,' he advised her.

She kept them open, though, and when he told her to lift, did so. It was awkward because they were in such a small space; it meant she had to stretch her arms at an impossible, aching angle and hold the small body rock steady, while Gijs probed and poked and prodded. It seemed an age before he finally said quietly: 'Now,' and pulled with steady strength.

It was an ugly wound and it began to bleed at once. At a word from Gijs, Serena scrambled out to get his bag, just as the door opened and two policemen came in. She stood on one side then while the children were lifted out and laid on the floor on the other side of the room, and when Gijs said:

'Pass me the dressings, Serena,' she did so, then found the syringes and the ATS and drew it up. When she handed it to him he glanced down at her hands and said, 'You're badly scratched and there's a graze on your arm.' She looked in a surprised way at her filthy hands because she hadn't felt any pain and said rather stupidly, 'I'm very dirty.'

They put pads and bandages on the two children then and one of the policemen picked up the toddler and carried her outside. Of the girl there was no sign and when Serena asked: 'The mother? Has anyone told her?' Gijs nodded towards the second policeman. 'He's just off to fetch her now. Get into the car, you're coming with me to the hospital.'

'There's no need. . .' she began.

He picked up the boy. 'Do as I ask, Serena,' he commanded softly.

She sat in the back of the Bentley with the boy in her lap, with the police car, with the toddler inside, in front of them, sounding its siren and flashing its blue lamp.

The hospital was low-storied and built in the form of a wide V, and inside it was very like any other hospital she had been in. The procession she was following halted in Casualty and Serena found a quiet corner away from the little group round the children, wishing she hadn't come, because although Gijs had told her to come, he had apparently forgotten all about her. But he hadn't. After a few moments a nurse detached herself from the group and came towards her, drew her into one of the cubicles and looked carefully at her scratched hands and the graze, then cleaned them equally carefully. She went away again then, to return in a few minutes with a syringe.

'ATS?' queried Serena, and hoped it was the same in Dutch. Apparently it was, for the nurse nodded and smiled and then stood aside when a doctor came in—the doctor she had seen with Gijs. He smiled nicely at her and said in English: 'Your husband asked me to give you penicillin, Jonkvrouw van Amstel,' and plunged the needle in without ado. 'He says also if you will now go home—the police will take you, he will return later.'

He walked to the door with her and they shook hands and Serena, looking at herself for the first time, declared: 'My goodness, I should think I should go home! I need a bath, don't I—and some clean clothes.' She said goodbye and walked to where the little white police car was waiting. At home, in the cool, fragrant hall, she met Jaap's horrified look. She explained as best she could, stumbling over the awkward Dutch words because it was difficult to do so with the limited vocabulary at her disposal, but he understood enough and called to Lien who came hurrying from the kitchen, to bustle Serena upstairs, where she took off the disgusting dress and dirty sandals and ran a bath, commanding, in a motherly tone, that her mistress should get into it at once. She had frowned and tut-tutted over the scratches and graze and gone away, talking to herself, to reappear as Serena emerged from the bathroom with a tea tray and strict instructions to sit down at once and drink her tea and eat some of the delicious little biscuits Lien had just that minute taken from the oven.

It was nice being cosseted, even though she didn't feel in the least ill, only hurt because Gijs had had no time for her, and even as she thought it, she knew it was unfair because the children had, quite rightly, absorbed all his attention. She told herself bracingly that she was becoming selfish and spoilt, and the quicker she changed her ways the better. She finished her tea, did up her newly washed hair, spent a good deal of time on her face, and put on a new dress—a patterned voile of a pleasing shade of blue. It was almost five o'clock. Gijs might come home before he went to the surgery.

He didn't—he wasn't back by dinner time either. Serena waited for an hour and then, urged by Lien, ate hers, with a book propped up before her and the dogs to keep her company. It was almost ten o'clock when he came in quietly with a placid: 'Hullo there—sorry I couldn't let you know.'

She got up from the chair in which she had been curled. 'It didn't matter—you've been busy. I'll see about your dinner. Tell me, how are the children?'

'The little girl's all right—the clavicle was a clean break, and we excised the puncture wound—luckily it hadn't penetrated deeply. She's concussed but not deeply. The boy's more serious. We had to do an extensive excision of wound and open up a good deal to clear it of splinters. By some miracle it missed the bone, but the tissues are badly damaged. Still, he's young and tough. He's badly concussed, though.'

'Did you suture the wound or leave it open?' she asked.

'Open—I packed it with petroleum jelly gauze and sulpha powder.'

She nodded. 'Do you suppose it will heal by first intention?'

'Yes, I should imagine so.' He was smiling now. 'I told you how much I needed someone to listen to me, didn't I?'

She was at the door. 'Actually,' she said, 'if I were a really good wife, I should be in the kitchen, fetching your dinner. I've put the whisky out.'

She sat at the table with him while he ate and when he asked, gave him a lighthearted version of her own part in the afternoon's happenings. When she had finished, he observed: 'It was most fortunate that you were home. The girl lost her head.'

'She disappeared. Did anyone find her?'

He nodded. 'Yes, half dead with fright. I think she was under the impression that she would be sent to prison.'

'The poor mother. . .'

'Yes—her husband has left her and she's been trying to manage; too proud to ask for help. I've put someone on to that, they'll see to everything.' He passed his cup for more coffee. 'Was there any post?'

She got up and went to his study and brought back the little pile of letters, saying: 'I suppose they can't wait? Could I help?'

He smiled. 'Open them for me, there's a good girl, would you? You can throw out the circulars

and so on and I'll scribble notes on the rest and
Juffrouw Kingsma can deal with them in the morning.' He picked up a letter as he spoke and became
immersed in it, so Serena collected the dinner things
on to a tray and carried it away to the kitchen, then
went back to the dining-room to wish him good
night. He wasn't there. As she stood in the doorway,
she heard the Bentley whisper quietly away from
the front door and her eyes filled with childish tears;
he could have at least called out as he went or spared
a second to come and find her. She went up to bed
and lay awake until she heard the car turn the corner
of the *steeg* and sigh its way gently into the garage.
It was after half past one. After a few minutes she
put on her dressing gown and slippers; she would
go down and make him a hot drink; he would be
tired. She was almost at the bedroom door when she
heard him coming upstairs and go into his room. He
closed the door very quietly after him and the house
became silent again. Serena took off her dressing
gown again and got back into bed—it had been a
silly idea anyway, had he not said that he didn't like
her getting up at night? It was almost day before
she went to sleep.

At breakfast he was his own casual self. They had
taken their usual walk together and he had talked
about the children and asked her about her scratched
hands and praised her for her part in their rescue. It
was towards the end of the meal that he mentioned
that Tante Emilie would like her to go and have
coffee with her one morning soon.

Serena buttered a roll. 'Oh? Did she telephone? I
didn't know. . .'

'No, I saw her last night—briefly. There was a
note, delivered by hand, with the post you gave me.

It was from Adriana. She is at Tante Emilie's house for a day or two; she wanted to see me urgently, and we are such old friends. . .' He paused and Serena waited for him to continue, but he didn't, only looked at her thoughtfully as though he were deciding whether to tell her something or not. Not, she concluded, and murmured, for something to say, 'How nice,' at the same time longing to scream at him that she was tingling all over with a poisonous mixture of rage and jealousy and curiosity. She choked back these ill-bred feelings with a mighty effort and asked instead:

'Will you be late this evening?' and when he shook his head, reminded him: 'We have to go to the van Oppens for dinner, you know.' Doctor van Oppen lived in Dreishoor and she liked his wife. They would sit and gossip after dinner and the two men would smoke their pipes and discuss their work until Mevrouw van Oppen suggested more coffee or a drink, and then they would bid each other good night and Gijs would drive her home, talking of nothing in particular—and that, she thought savagely, would be another day.

But not quite, for when they got home that evening, instead of wishing her good night and going to his study, Gijs said: 'There's something I want to tell you—if you're not too tired?'

Serena went before him into the study and sat down in the smaller of the two easy chairs drawn up to the empty hearth. She hadn't spoken because she was speechless with the dread that he was going to remind her of his words when he had offered to marry her; that they should tell each other if they fell in love with someone else. She had all of the long day in which to think about his sudden departure the night before and he had made no secret of whom he had met, although he had given her no reason. . .but then, she had argued to herself, why should he? She might be his wife, but had they not married on the understanding that they were to be good friends with no deeper feelings involved? She had added and discarded conjectures for hours and had always reached the same total, that whatever he had said, he was in love with Adriana even though she had chosen to marry Laurens, and she——Serena had used her imagination here to embroider the story——knowing Gijs's feelings for her, had summoned him and he had gone at once, without so much as a good night. Perhaps, Serena had thought rather wildly, Adriana had changed her mind again, and didn't want to marry Laurens after all and had sent for Gijs so that she could tell him this. She sat very still, her folded hands on the silken lap of her dress, very aware of Gijs sitting opposite her. He seemed in no hurry to speak, so in the end, edgy with nerves, she remarked:

'It was a pleasant evening, wasn't it? I like Mevrouw van Oppen—she asked me to call her Wil. She gave me the recipe for that Bavarian Cream, and. . .'

'Serena, you're babbling,' said her husband, and smiled at her with a faintly puzzled amusement. 'I was going to tell you why I went to see Adriana last night,' his grey eyes searched hers. 'Perhaps you already know.'

'She's ill?' asked Serena, hope dying hard.

He shook her head. 'No, her health is perfect. I thought you might have guessed, or heard. . .'

It was, she discovered, more than she could stand; she was so steeped in her own imagined version of their meeting that she answered quite sharply: 'Yes, of course I've guessed,' and jumped to her feet. 'Do you mind if we don't talk any more now? I—I've got such a bad headache.'

She made for the door, not looking at him at all; she barely heard his quiet, 'Good night, Serena,' as she closed the door behind her.

In her room she took off her shoes and curled up in the centre of the bed, her head a whirlpool of forebodings and memories and ragged thoughts without beginning or ending. Horrid, vivid flash-backs unfolded themselves before her eyes and the most vivid of them of the occasion when she had asked him if Adriana was his girl and he had said 'Lies, all lies,' and she had actually believed him. It all fitted so well—it was Adriana he loved, this quiet man who never showed his feelings to her, and when Laurens had stolen a march on him, he hadn't really cared what happened, and because he was kind and had felt sorry for her and liked her, and his own future was wrecked, he had suggested that they could do worse than marry each other. After all, she told herself bitterly, it couldn't have mattered to him whom he married. Just as it hadn't mattered to her. She choked on a sob; she'd made a fine mess of things. In the morning, when she felt better, she would talk to him. It shouldn't be too difficult, for he didn't know that she loved him, and as long as he didn't find that out... She got off the bed and started to undress, walking around the room, dropping things and leaving them where they fell.

But once in bed, she couldn't sleep for thinking about the morning and what she would say, getting very muddled and more and more confused as the night wore on. She would, of course, return to

England; she would have to use some of the money Gijs gave her so generously, but she didn't think he would mind. She would drive the Mini to Schipol and leave it there, then stay quietly out of his way until everything was nicely settled with as little fuss as possible. There was his good name to consider. On this high-minded resolution, she at last fell asleep.

She overslept; Gijs had gone by the time she got downstairs, to eat a solitary breakfast with only the dogs for company. Still resolved to carry out her good intentions, although she was, in broad daylight, a little vague as to what exactly she would do, she attended to her household chores, took the dogs for a long walk along the *gracht* which encircled the town and arrived home to find a message from Gijs to say that he wouldn't be home for lunch. So she had a second lonely meal, and was just debating what she should do to fill the time before Gijs came home, when the telephone rang. It was Tante Emilie—her voice, coming threadily over the wire, inviting her with more warmth than usual to go and have tea that afternoon. 'Laurens is away at The Hague,' she explained, 'and Adriana has gone home, poor girl, so I am a little lonely.'

Serena agreed readily enough. It would help to pass the afternoon; anything would be better than giving herself the leisure to think. She remembered then that they were to dine at Renesse that evening, unless Gijs came home early there would be no time to talk before they went. It would have to be when they returned. Rehearsing, for the hundredth time, what she would say to him, she went up to her room to tidy herself.

Tante Emilie was in the garden, sitting in the shade of the trees, away from the house. She wel-

comed Serena with slightly more warmth than the
cold politeness she usually accorded her, and began
to talk at once about the wedding, the guests,
Serena's wedding dress and the unfortunate circumstances which prevented her and Gijs going on a
honeymoon. She enlarged upon this theme for some
minutes until the tea tray was brought out, a diver-
sion which Serena welcomed with relief. They were
sipping the beverage when Jonkvrouw van Amstel
changed the subject with startling abruptness.

'You know that Laurens is going to America?'

Serena put down her cup. She was surprised, but
that was all, she didn't care in the least where
Laurens went. She said carefully: 'No, I didn't.'

'I am surprised. Gijs has known for some weeks,
but of course, he would hardly have wished to discuss it with you.'

'Why ever not?' Serena wanted to know.

Her hostess's look was a mixture of curiosity,
triumph and pure mischief.

'It is still painful for him to do so, I imagine. He
and Adriana...' She left the sentence in the air,
to exasperate Serena. 'She and Laurens are ideally
suited, of course, and they will be happy,' she gave
this opinion with a certain smugness, and turned a
sharp eye upon Serena, 'though I have no doubt that
Gijs could win her back without any difficulty at
all, although of course he is now hindered from
doing so, is he not, my dear?'

Serena said nothing because her tongue was doing
that most unlikely of things, cleaving to the roof of
her mouth, which gave her hostess the opportunity
to say: 'Laurens has a very good post in Pittsburg.'

Serena would have liked to drink some tea, anything to delay having to speak, but she felt sure that

her cup and saucer would rattle in her trembling hands, she crossed her feet, admired her shoes, drew a deep breath and asked with commendable calm:

'What about the practice?'

Tante Emilie shrugged her shoulders. 'Gijs knows plenty of men who would be delighted to step into Laurens's shoes.'

'Gijs—last night. . .'

'Came at once,' said her companion with satisfaction. 'Of course we left them alone—it was something she and Gijs had to decide together.'

Serena, controlling her hands, drank her tea. And what was to happen to her—to them both? Sooner or later she would have to know, and it might as well be now; it would be far better if she knew the whole story before she saw Gijs. She winced at the thought, and Tante Emilie, who had been watching her, said with faint malice: 'Gijs seems very fond of you, my dear.'

Serena caught the malice although it puzzled her. 'I should like to see Adriana,' she stated.

'The dear child is in Amsterdam—with her family, you know—she went early this morning. They have a large house in Amstelveen. . .' She enlarged upon the house, its garden and its furnishings at some length, but Serena, who was nothing if not tenacious, said: 'Then perhaps you will give me her address; I should like to go and see her.'

Her hostess paused. 'Why, yes, of course you shall have her address, my dear. You could drive up and see her.' And she wrote it down, giving precise directions and advice as to how to get to Amstelveen and which part of the town to avoid. Serena, listening to her meticulous instructions, felt ashamed of her ill-feeling towards her hostess. She took her leave, telling herself that she had misjudged the lady after all.

Gijs was late home. He barely had time to shower and change before setting out for Renesse, and once there the evening lengthened out to so late an hour that by the time they were home again, Serena knew that it would be hopeless to try to talk to him. Tomorrow, she promised herself as she wished him good night and paused on the stairs when he told her:

'I'll be in Utrecht all day, Serena. Will you be all right on your own? I shall leave very early—with any luck I shall be back for dinner.'

So that would be another day gone by—he would be tired after such a long day, it would hardly be fair to expect him to discuss their future. She told him quietly that she would be perfectly all right, and resolved then and there to go to Amstelveen. It was a splendid opportunity to get to the bottom of Tante Emilie's hints.

She didn't enjoy the drive to Amstelveen; the road was empty enough as far as Vlaardingen so that she had plenty of opportunity to think, and her thoughts weren't happy ones. She hadn't seen Gijs that morning, although she had heard the Bentley steal from the garage just after six, and when she had gone downstairs she had found an envelope on her breakfast plate with a note inside, written in Gijs's small, immaculate handwriting: 'Buy yourself something pretty.' It was wrapped round a little wad of money. He was, she told herself, the most kind and considerate of men; the thought was followed by another one, one of which she was instantly ashamed; he could have been easing his conscience.

It was getting on for noon by the time she reached Amstelveen for she had gone the wrong way twice and had had to stop to look at the road signs besides. The house was one in an avenue of pleasant villas, unimaginative as to build but decidedly prosperous-looking. She parked the Mini neatly and walked up the short front path and rang the door bell. She had to ring again before anyone answered it and when the woman at last came to the door Serena had the impression that she had been expecting her, but she must have been wrong in this; the woman had difficulty in understanding Serena's frugal Dutch and when she did at last reply it was to shake her head and say: 'The Juffrouw has left, this morning—early.'

'Where to?' asked Serena, ever dogged.

'Friesland, north of Leeuwarden—many kilometres.'

Serena, who had spent a long time poring over maps and mileages when she had had the Mini, spent a few minutes turning kilometres into miles—miles didn't seem so far, but even when she had done that it was still ninety miles away, and that was only to Leeuwarden. She could never get there and back again to Zierikzee before Gijs got back in the evening. In the Bentley with Gijs driving it would have been easy enough—besides, she didn't know the road and the woman, when she questioned her further, wasn't disposed to be helpful. She thanked her and went back to the car, feeling deflated.

She got home again about three o'clock without having stopped for lunch.

'There's a tray ready for you in the kitchen, *Mevrouw*,' Jaap told her. 'If you like to go into the house I'll fetch it along to you—unless you lunched on the way?'

'No, Jaap. But don't stop your gardening. I'll take it with me as I go.'

She carried it through the house and set it on the dining-table. Its contents looked delicious, but she wasn't hungry. She fed German and Gus with wafers of *rookworst* and ham, feeling a little guilty about it, drank the coffee in the thermos jug and then carried it back to the kitchen and went up to her room. The dogs went with her; the three of them got on to the bed and presently went to sleep.

It was tea time when she wakened. Gijs didn't come in until eight o'clock, when they ate a dinner which Lien had miraculously managed to hold back for an hour without ruining any of it, and over it, Gijs told her about his day at some concourse or other; Serena listened carefully, asking intelligent questions and paying attention to his answers and all the while longing to say: 'Gijs, why can't we talk—really talk?' for he seemed remote, and getting more remote all the time. Over coffee she said:

'There's a great deal of post for you today, shall I fetch it?' and when he said that no, he would read it presently, she saw her last chance of saying something sliding away until the next day, and who knew, he might be away from home again. Rendered reckless by frustration, she asked suddenly, her tongue saying the words she really didn't wish to utter:

'Gijs, were you ever in love with Adriana?'

He leaned back in his chair and smiled a little and said lazily: 'What man wouldn't be in love with such a pretty creature at some time or other in his life?'

Which was no answer at all, so that she tried again, her voice a little too high and loud. 'Are you still in love with her?'

His expression didn't change. The smile was still there, only his eyes were half closed so that she was unable to read their expression.

'You're not serious, dear girl?'

And that wasn't an answer either. She nodded. 'How can you bear to let her go?'

He was filling his pipe and didn't look at her. 'Who told you that Adriana was going away?'

'Your aunt—Tante Emilie. I had tea with her two days ago. She hinted. . . Gijs, did Adriana ask you to go and see her?'

'Yes.' His voice was bland.

'You went to make her change her mind?'

'Yes.'

'Did you succeed?' Her voice wasn't loud any more, but a small dry whisper.

'Yes, dear girl.' He leaned back a little further in his chair, his eyes still half shut. 'Aren't you going to ask me what was the reason for my asking?'

'I know.' Serena was proud of her voice; in her ears it sounded unflurried and calm, so it was all the more infuriating therefore when he remarked placidly, 'Are you being just a little over-hasty?'

She eyed him across the table. He didn't look as though he cared a button for her opinion, over-hasty or otherwise. She had her mouth open to say so when there was a hammering on the front door knocker and Gijs went to open it, calling to Jaap to stay where he was in the kitchen, as he did so. Serena heard him talking to someone at the door and then he was back again, with Laurens.

He greeted her with a mixture of gay charm and apology which at any other time might have flattered her, but now his: 'Hullo, Serena, have you forgiven me for my bad behaviour at the surgery?' left her unmoved. She got to her feet and smiled with something of an effort. 'Yes, of course, I'd forgotten all about it. Will you have some coffee?'

'No, thanks—I'm only here for a few minutes. Adriana wants to see Gijs and nothing would do but that I should fetch him myself.'

Serena said slowly: 'I thought Adriana was in Friesland.'

Laurens had already turned away, ready to leave. He said over his shoulder:

'Friesland? You've been dreaming—she's still at Mother's house. She certainly wouldn't go all that way.' He laughed across to Gijs, standing by the door. 'I've had to stand down for Gijs, you know.'

The two men took their leave of her and she supposed that she had answered them sensibly because, beyond a casual good night, they said nothing. As the front door closed behind them she found herself wondering how it was that Laurens could be so cheerful at the thought of losing Adriana to Gijs, and that was another thing—why had Tante Emilie told her that Adriana was in Amstelveen and then, when she had got there, why had the woman who had answered the door told her that Adriana was in Friesland? She could think of no sensible answer and after roaming round the house doing nothing, she went and sat down with an open book on her lap; she would read quietly until Gijs came back and they would discuss everything with calm and sense. She read the same page several times, telling herself that he wouldn't be more than half an hour.

But he didn't come back in half an hour. Serena waited for another half an hour and then another and finally went up to bed. She lay awake a very long time, but Gijs still hadn't come.

He greeted her with his usual placid friendliness the next morning, and without giving her a chance to take the conversation into her own hands, talked about everything and anything but themselves. They were seated at breakfast and she was still trying to frame a sentence urgent enough to engage his attention, when he looked up briefly from his post to ask:

'How would you like to go to England?'

She got up to let Gus into the garden and kept her back to him as she answered steadily: 'Yes, I should like that. Could—could it be arranged easily, without anyone. . .' She was interrupted by the telephone. It was a long call. When Gijs came back Lien was in the room with some household query and Serena said with determined brightness: 'Will you be home to lunch, Gijs?'

He thought he might. At the door he turned to look at her. 'I want to talk to you, my dear,' he told her as he went out.

The morning went on leaden feet. Serena occupied it with unnecessary tasks, getting in Lien's way until that poor woman suggested that Serena might like to go to the butcher and order the meat and call in at the grocer for the particular brand of mustard Gijs preferred. Serena went willingly; it would distract her thoughts, which, having been given full rein since breakfast, were in such a state of muddled truth and fiction that she no longer knew which was which.

When she arrived home Gijs was already there. His bag was on the table in the hall and as she shut the door he came downstairs, not hurrying, although she was struck by the sense of urgency he conveyed, so strong was it that she began to apologize. 'I didn't know you would be home early. I went to the shops—I won't be a minute.'

She started for the kitchen, but he intercepted her with one leisurely stride, taking her packages and tossing them on to the table, and unleashing Gus, who, delighted to see German again, ran to meet him in the garden. She felt his arm on her shoulders as he led her through the door beneath the stairs, past his study, to the sitting-room at the back of the house. Gijs stopped in the open door leading to the garden and turned her round to face him. When he spoke his voice was casual; he could have been talking about the weather.

'My dear, it seems to me that things aren't turning out quite as I—we had hoped. We are friends, are we not? and yet we seem unable to understand each other. . .my fault, I know. I've been busy—too busy. Life must have been dull for you these last few weeks, but I promise you an end to that—there will be changes. . .' He looked all of a sudden withdrawn, and Serena, who had put her own interpretation on his words, said impulsively: 'How can you bear it? It's worse than you thought, isn't it? Is Adriana going with Laurens to America—I mean when he goes?'

He looked at her with faint surprise. 'I believe so. Serena. . .'

'They're going to be married. . .?' She stared at him as she spoke and saw that his face now had no expression upon it at all. Suddenly she couldn't go on; she didn't want to hear, to have to put into words, all her unhappy, hopeless thoughts. She would go away, she thought, quickly, without talking about it. She could leave a note for Gijs telling him that she didn't want to be married any more and he would be free for his Adriana, for it was obvious to her that Laurens would stand no chance at all if Gijs were free. Adriana had taken him as second choice and because Tante Emilie had set her heart on it. She didn't know about Laurens, whether he loved Adriana or not, and she didn't care.

'You're not listening,' she heard Gijs's quiet voice cutting through her busy thoughts. 'Never mind. I've chosen the wrong moment, haven't I? But there's time enough for what I have to say. Let's have lunch. Isn't it this evening that we're having dinner with the Wisselaars?'

She followed his lead; lunch passed off surprisingly pleasantly, with no more awkward questions requiring answers. They kept to trivialities while behind Serena's bleak, lovely face, her brain seethed. Gijs had only left the house five minutes, and she was at the telephone, asking the exchange to get the number of Doctor van Elven, in Richmond.

Gijs was home for tea, although late. As he joined her in the garden he apologized for his delay. 'A telephone call, just as I was leaving the hospital,' he explained. She noticed how bright his eyes were as he spoke, even though his face wore its habitual calm expression. She passed him his tea, her imagination, rioting around inside her head, had already supplied the caller—Adriana, of course. She took an angry breath and choked over her tea, then was forced to suffer the humiliation of having him pat her on the back while she struggled to get her breath.

Serena dressed very carefully that evening; Mevrouw Wisselaar was the *Burgemeester*'s wife, a lady with an extensive wardrobe, the reason Serena gave herself for putting on a new and very expensive little dress she had bought at a boutique she had discovered in Veere when she had driven herself there one afternoon. It was a peach pink chiffon, pleated and cunningly cut with long full sleeves and little pearl buttons fastening the deep cuffs. She put on the ruby earrings and the kid sandals she had bought in England before she married, picked up the matching handbag and took a quick look at herself in the mirror. The whole effect, she was bound to admit, was most successful, only she must remember to smile.

Gijs was waiting for her in the sitting-room when she went in. He looked her over without haste and said finally: 'Delightful—I hope I'm the one you want to impress.'

Of course it was, but she had no intention of letting him know that. What good could it possibly do—and anyway, he was only being kind and polite as he unfailingly was. She said flippantly: 'Well, actually, no. It's for the *Burgemeester's* wife, she has smashing clothes, you know, and I felt like competing.'

He smiled. 'I imagine you'll win easily. Is there to be anyone else there?'

Serena told him as they went out to the car, and during the short drive she chatted, feverishly, about this and that, terrified that he would start to talk about her going to England. But he made no mention of it; it was as though he had forgotten his suggestion, and once at their host's house, she saw very little of him for the entire evening, for at dinner she sat between an important lawyer from The Hague and an elderly and charming *dominee* from Veere; both gentlemen seemed bent on improving her knowledge of their country and she rose from the table, her head reeling under the facts and figures and statistics they had fired at her.

To avoid a silence on the way home she told Gijs
about the elderly gentlemen and had even managed
to laugh with him about it and go on to talk about
the evening in a quite gay manner. Parting from him
in the hall of their home, it struck her forcibly that
this would be the last time she would do that.
Tomorrow she would be in England, at Sarah's
house, and he. . .he would be with Adriana, perhaps.
She wondered if he and Laurens would quarrel about
Adriana, or would Gijs arrange everything quietly
and competently, as he had arranged? She forced
herself to stop thinking and lifted her face and presented a cheek for Gijs to kiss, then turned away to
go upstairs; she was on the bottom step when she
was arrested by his voice, very casual and drawling.

'I should have told you sooner, Serena. I have to
leave very early tomorrow morning—another meeting—an important one to me. I shall be gone before
you are up. What were your plans for tomorrow?'

'Plans? I—I. . .' she had been taken by surprise.
'I don't know. I expect I shall take the car. I hope
your meeting will be a success.'

His quiet voice followed her up the stairs. 'It will
be,' he said.

CHAPTER NINE

SERENA heard Gijs leave just after six. She had had a wretched night and several times she had been tempted to discard her plans; to go and talk to him, to see Adriana, Laurens even, anything rather than go away. There were so many small reasons why she should stay, too. They had begun to matter to her—his parents, of whom she had become very fond, Gus, whom she loved, the ever-increasing circle of friends and last but by no means least, the lovely old house and the bustling little town. Life without these things, and above all, without Gijs, did not bear thinking about. She wept a little and then dried her tears quickly, telling herself that giving way to self-pity would do no good at all. Dressed, and with her bag packed, she crept downstairs to the garage where she left her bag in the Mini, then went back to put the letter she had written to Gijs in his study, and then to the kitchen.

Lien was already up, and Serena, who had anticipated this, embarked on a long story about going to visit someone a long way away and it was such a nice day it seemed a good idea to go early.

Saying good-bye to Gus and German was hard. Serena hadn't realized how hard when she had laid her plans, nor had she envisaged the wrench she would experience as she said good-bye to Lien and Jaap with a cheerfulness which sat ill upon her poor white face. She went round to the garage, trying not to look back at the house and doing so despite all

her resolution. She got into the Mini, her throat thick
with the tears she was determined not to shed, and
backed it into the *steeg*, then drove slowly past the
house, remembering to wave to Lien who was still
standing in the doorway.

There was a fine rain falling when Serena's taxi
drew up outside the van Elvens' house in Richmond.
It spattered down gently on to the pink linen dress
and jacket she was wearing and on to the small straw
hat which matched them; an unsuitable outfit in
which to run away, she had known that when she
had put them on, but they looked gay and carefree,
and she had the childish idea that they might cheer
her spirits. They had done nothing of the sort; she
watched the taxi drive off and then rang the bell in
a state of near panic. Now that she was here she
wondered what she should say to Sarah, for she
hadn't told her a great deal over the telephone—
perhaps she wouldn't ask. She had been a fool to
come. She half turned from the door, but it was too
late, Alice had opened it, to greet her smilingly and
take her bag as she ushered her into the hall, and
now it was certainly too late because Sarah was
coming through a door, looking more beautiful
than ever.

'Serena, how lovely to see you!' she kissed her
warmly. 'Come in, my dear.'

She opened the sitting-room door as she spoke
and Serena went past her into the room. She had
forgotten how kind Sarah was, as kind as she was
beautiful; she would tell her everything and ask her
advice—there would only be the two of them; Hugo
wouldn't be home until the evening or late afternoon.

She was wrong. Hugo van Elven was there, standing with his back to the empty fireplace, and beside

him stood Gijs, his hands in his pockets, very much at his ease.

Serena lost her breath, caught it again and turned, intent on escape, but Sarah was behind her and had shut the door and was leaning against it. 'Presently,' thought Serena tiredly, 'I shall be able to sort this out,' and walked on strangely shaky legs a few steps forward as Hugo came across the room to meet her. He took her hand and smiled and said: 'Dear little Serena, we seem to have been waiting a long time.' He looked over her shoulder and exchanged a glance with his wife, who opened the door. Serena hardly noticed them go, although she heard the door shut behind them.

The impulse to rush across the room straight into Gijs's arms was very great, but she resisted it because she wasn't sure why he was there, nor, for that matter, if he would welcome such a demonstration. He could be in London for some reason connected with his work—she had to know. She swallowed from a dry mouth and asked flatly: 'Why are you here?' She was pulling and tugging at her quite expensive handbag with no thought as to the damage she was causing.

For someone so unhurried in his movements, Gijs moved with surprising speed. The misused handbag was taken from her grasp and her hands taken in his.

'Dearest heart, where else should I be but where you are?'

Her heart threatened to choke her. She stared at his tie, a nice grey silk one; a small piece of her stunned brain approved of it. She kept her eyes steadily upon it and asked: 'How did—how could you possibly know?'

'My darling, Sarah telephoned me yesterday evening.'

Her beautiful eyes left the tie and flew to his face. She said on a surging breath: 'Well—well, how absolutely beastly of her! I left you a letter.'

'Yes? I thought perhaps you might. And don't think badly of Sarah. Do you remember that I told you once that one day I would tell you about her and Hugo? I think this is the moment.' He had released her hands and put his arms around her, holding her away a little so that he could see her face. 'When Hugo and Sarah married, she didn't love him—she had been—er—jilted and he caught her on the rebound. She ran away too, it took Hugo more than a week to find her. She is far too fond of you—and me—to let history repeat itself. So she telephoned me.'

Serena's eyes were back on his tie. 'She could have made an awful mistake. How did she know that I—how did she know anything?'

His voice was calmly reasonable. 'Well, my darling, she knew that I love you, just as your parents know.'

She looked at him then, the colour rushing into her pale face. 'Mother and Father—I don't under-stand—and Sarah. . .' She thought it over while her eyes searched his. She said at length: 'But you didn't tell me.'

'You didn't want to know, not at first, did you, my dearest dear? Your lovely head was still full of Laurens. You had to empty it of him before you could even notice me, and just when I was beginning to think that you had discovered that it was I and not Laurens you loved, you chose to stuff your head with a great deal of nonsense which, most unfortunately, made sense.'

It was like unravelling wool; she caught hold of the nearest conversational strand and pulled gently. 'I don't understand. Tante Emilie—she told me that day I went to tea that you and Adriana—that it was you, even though she and Laurens are going to get married, and when I asked you you said you'd been in love with her. You went to see her that evening and you didn't come home until half past one in the morning, and then Laurens came to fetch you.'

'And I tried to tell you, my adorable, pig-headed, addle-pated wife. Adriana is going to America with Laurens, you know that, but she may not go without being vaccinated. For some reason she had never been done as a child and she was terrified to the point of hysteria. She made such a fuss when Laurens attempted to vaccinate her that he gave up and she sent a note round asking me to do it. I persuaded her to have it done, but she didn't screw up the courage until the evening Laurens came for me. Do you not remember that he told you that he was having to stand aside for me?'

Serena gave a sniff because she wasn't sure if she was going to laugh or cry. She said pettishly, 'I thought he meant that you and Adriana—how ridiculous!' She sniffed again, wild laughter bubbling up inside her, warring with tears. She was still undecided which should win when Gijs solved the problem for her; he kissed her with such thoroughness and at such length that by the time he had finished she had forgotten everything else, or almost everything. Despite the kiss she persisted: 'But Tante Emilie—she told me that you and Adriana—that you loved her, and I thought that if I went away—

I thought that perhaps you had married me because you couldn't marry her and I was out on a limb anyway, and it wouldn't have mattered,' she drew a breath which ended in a sob. 'If you read my letter, you would see what I mean,' she ended, aware that she hadn't made herself very clear.

Gijs kissed her again, taking his time about it. 'I very much doubt it, my darling.' He sounded as though he was laughing, but he must have understood at least some of the half-finished sentences, obscure references and pure conjecture, for he added: 'Dearest Serena, what a lot of mistaken thinking you have been doing.' He sounded very comforting, just as his arms, holding her tightly now, were comforting. Serena, her voice muffled by his shoulder and still intent on getting everything quite clear, tried again. 'Tante Emilie told me. . .'

'Tante Emilie seems to have had a lot to say and none of it to a good purpose. She is old-fashioned, prejudiced and a doting mother, but above all she is obsessed by the family. A very long time ago, when I was a young man and Adriana was an even younger woman, I fell in love with her—I fell out of love within six weeks or so as one does at that age, but Tante Emilie decided that it would be a splendid thing if we were to marry. It was a bitter disappointment to her when I showed no desire to do any such thing; you can imagine how pleased she was when Laurens, years later, decided that Adriana was the girl for him, but then he met you, my darling, and you are very beautiful, you know, and he is susceptible to beautiful girls. Poor Tante Emilie; you were the stumbling block to all her plans. I don't think she could quite forgive you, so she took a pretty revenge by allowing you to believe that Adriana and

I were still in love with each other, a piece of nonsense Adriana will be the first to disclaim.'

Serena gave a weak chuckle. 'Oh, Gijs, darling Gijs, what a stupid creature I've been—vaccinating Adriana, and all the while I thought...I went to Amstelveen to see her.'

Her husband took this unexpected turn in the conversation in his stride.

'Tell me about it, dearest.' Which she did with a fair amount of coherence and then lifted her lovely, faintly tearstained face to his so that he was forced to remark: 'I can't blame Laurens in the least for falling for you—I did myself, the moment I set eyes on you.'

'In the front hall of Queen's,' added Serena happily. 'Did you really? I didn't fall in love with you, you know, although I knew you were there.'

'Yes? I made up my mind to marry you on the way up to Laurens's room. I knew that it would take time and patience, but I had plenty of both, and I have found that if one has patience enough one gets what one wants in the end.'

He smiled down at her and she wondered how she could ever have imagined that he was casual and easy-going, for just at that moment he looked very alert and his eyes, no longer hidden by their drooping lids, had a glint in them which set her heart tripping over itself in a most disturbing fashion.

'How nice,' he observed slowly, 'that we don't have to get married, and how equally nice that we can go home together.'

Serena snuggled her head a little deeper into his shoulder. 'In time for evening surgery?' she inquired flippantly.

She was crushed in a gentle hug. 'Father is taking

over for this evening—he'll take over for a week while we have a honeymoon, too. Shall I tell you where we're going?'

She nodded. 'Though I don't mind if we don't have one.'

He ignored this remark. 'Scotland. Hugo has a tiny cottage in Wester Ross. We can go when we like.'

'It sounds lovely! When shall we go? Oh, Gijs, I'm so happy I think I'm going to cry. Laurens told me once that you were very good at letting girls cry on your shoulder.'

'Not girls, dearest—just you, and later on, our daughters.'

Serena said gently: 'No, little boys, all like you.'

'There is such a thing as compromise, my love,' said Gijs on a laugh. 'How about an equal number of each?'

She sniffed too late, a tear trickled down her cheek. 'Oh, Gijs, I do love you.'

'And I love you, my darling.' He kissed her again by way of proof. 'I believe that I shall tell you so very frequently for the rest of our lives. In the meantime, though, I think we might allow Hugo and Sarah to return, don't you? Hugo is waiting to open the champagne and Sarah and Alice have concocted a magnificent lunch—besides, we haven't a great deal of time in which to catch our plane.'

'What plane?' asked Serena, her thoughts already flying ahead, in Zierikzee.

'I've booked on the five o'clock flight, I thought it would be nice if we had dinner together in our own home.'

'Super!' uttered Serena, and turned a bright smiling face to Sarah and Hugo as they came in.

*   *   *

It was dark before they were back in Zierikzee. Gijs had driven fast from Schipol and they hadn't talked very much because there wasn't any need, only as they crossed the stretch of water between Oude Tonge and Zijpe, and saw Schouwen-Duivenland before them, Serena said: 'I can't see Zierikzee, but I know it's near. I'm so happy!'

Gijs' hand rested briefly on her knee. 'My dear heart, did you really think that I should allow anything else? You are my life, without you there would be nothing.'

They tore along the empty road across the island, to slow down at the towering gateway and pass beneath it and into the quiet of the Oudehaven. Gijs wasn't hurrying now. They passed the Mondragon, its lights cheerful in the darkened town, and turned across the head of the canal and so to the other side—the side where home was. As Gijs drew up, Serena could hear German's staccato bark and Gus's excited treble, and when he opened the door, the two dogs hurled themselves at them in an ecstatic welcome, and Lien and Jaap came hurrying from the kitchen. They were standing, all of them together, when the telephone rang, and Gijs, his arm in hers, crossed to answer it. She stood within the circle of his arm and heard him say:

'I have her here, Mama, safe with me,' and when he put down the receiver she said in a surprised voice: 'Your mother knew!'

'Yes, darling. I had to ask Father to take the surgery, you see, and Mama is good at putting two and two together.'

'She must think I've been an awful fool.'

Her husband's arms drew her close. 'No, she doesn't.'

'And you—what do you think?' inquired Serena.

'Come into the sitting-room and I'll tell you,' said Gijs. 'It may take some time.'

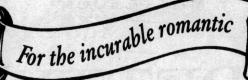

MILLS & BOON®

BETTY NEELS

COLLECTOR'S EDITION

If you have missed any of the previously published titles in the Betty Neels Collector's Edition our Customer Care department will be happy to advise you of titles currently in stock. Alternatively send in a large stamped addressed envelope and we will be pleased to provide you with full details by post. Please send your SAE to:

Betty Neels Collector's Edition
Customer Care Department
Eton House
18-24 Paradise Road
Richmond
Surrey TW9 1SR

Customer Care Direct Line - 0181 288 2888